Christine Merrill lives on a farm in Wisconsin, USA, with her husband, two sons and too many pets—all of whom would like her to get off the computer so they can check their email. She has worked by turns in theatre costuming and as a librarian. Writing historical romance combines her love of good stories and fancy dress with her ability to stare out of the window and make stuff up.

A KISS AWAY FROM SCANDAL

Christine Merrill

MILLS & BOON

To Clara Bloczynski: there can be only one.

Chapter One

'I have a problem.'

In Gregory Drake's experience, most conversations began with exactly those words. But that was to be expected, given the unusual nature of his profession.

Gregory fixed things.

Not in the usual sense. Watchmakers fixed watches. Tinkers mended kettles. But Gregory was not a tradesman as much as a student of human nature. He fixed lives. When members of the upper classes were confronted with a situation that was difficult, embarrassing, or simply tedious, they came to him.

He made their problems go away. Quickly, quietly and without another word.

It was why he was welcome in the reading rooms at Boodle's and White's and most of the other clubs in London. He could claim membership in none of them. But he was so often found in attendance at them, sharing hushed conversations with important people, that no one dared to ask the reason for his presence. Though society might see him as an underling, even its most august members kept a respectful distance from him, not wanting to embarrass their friends. More importantly, they did not want to annoy the fellow who could be counted on to rescue them when trouble arose.

Today, Gregory stretched his legs towards the fireplace to warm the January chill from his bones. Then he looked expectantly to the man in the opposite chair. 'Does your problem involve a woman?' Until his recent marriage, James Leggett had been a well-known rake who courted scandal almost as actively as he chased the females that embroiled him in it.

At this, Leggett laughed. 'It involves several women. But none in the way you probably expect, given my reputation.'

'If not an *affaire de coeur*, then what could it be?'

'It concerns my wife's family,' Leggett said,

with a sigh. 'Lovely ladies, all. But there are far too many of them for one man to handle.'

'That is why you are speaking to me,' Gregory said, with an understanding nod.

'The branches of the Strickland family tree are so full of women that it is all but dead. My darling Faith has two sisters and a grandmother.'

'The Dowager Countess of Comstock,' Gregory supplied, to prove he was well aware of the circumstances. 'The Earl had no brothers and all three of his sons are dead. But, I understand the Crown has found an heir to the earldom. There is a cousin of some sort, several times removed and living in America.'

Leggett nodded. 'This leaves the ladies in a somewhat precarious position.'

In a just society, it would not. In Gregory's opinion, men should be required by law to make provision for the future of female relatives and property should be divided equitably amongst all siblings, regardless of sex. But no one gave a damn for the opinion of a fellow without inherited wealth, nor did it make sense to argue reform with a man who had benefitted from the current system. Instead, he described the situation at hand. 'The last Earl left them a pittance and the ladies fear that the new one will take even that away from them.'

'It is not as if they will starve in the streets,' Leggett said quickly. 'I will provide for them, if no one else shall. But they are worried. The heir has called for an audit of the entail to be completed before he arrives.'

Suddenly everything became clear. 'I take it there might be some problems in the accounting?'

'The Countess is a delightful woman,' Leggett said with a smile. 'Charming and sweet-tempered, but a trifle foolish. She could not resist keeping up the appearance of wealth where it no longer existed.'

'She has been selling off the family jewels,' Gregory said. Women of titled men sometimes grew so used to the baubles they wore that they thought of them as personal property and not things meant by law to be passed down the generations, from one peer to the next.

'Nothing as dire as that. It seems she's pillaged furniture, paintings and assorted bric-a-brac.' Leggett held his hands wide to indicate the variety in the theft. 'It is all quite random. The only record of the sales exists in her faulty memory.'

'You need someone to search the Lombard merchants for the missing items.'

'With a dray and draught horses if necessary. God knows how much is missing. Buy it all back at my expense,' Leggett said, closing his eyes in resignation. 'And finish before the arrival of the new Comstock. There are rumours of rough seas between here and Philadelphia, but weather will not forestall discovery once his man of business arrives. With two sisters yet to be married, my wife is terrified that any scandal will spoil their reputation.'

'I have contacts in the industry that might help me with retrieval,' Gregory assured him. 'You are not the first to come to me with such a problem. Once I am on the case, it will be sorted in no time.'

'But in the past, you did not have to contend with the Strickland sisters.' Leggett gave him a rueful grimace.

Gregory countered with what he hoped was a reassuring smile. 'If they are named for the three theological virtues, how much trouble can they be?'

'How much trouble? As much as they can manage, I suspect.' There was something in the quirk of his lips that was not quite a smile. It spoke of bitter experience. Then, his face gentled. 'My Faith is a continual delight, of course. But she has a will of iron.'

'The shield and bulwark of the family?'

'Rather,' Leggett replied. 'She is the eldest and used to running things. I am removing her from the equation, for my pleasure and her piece of mind. A month in Italy will leave you free to do the work she would take on herself, if I allowed her to.'

'That is probably for the best,' Gregory said cautiously. 'And the other two?'

'Charity is the youngest,' Leggett said.

'A sweet child, I am sure.'

'She is no child. She is fully nineteen and cold comfort, at best.' Leggett glanced about him to be sure no one heard his candid assessment. 'A whey-faced girl with a mind as sharp as a razor and a tongue to match. She will be a great help, if you can persuade her to put down her books and leave the library. But she has the brain of a chess master and, if she decides to work against you, your battle is lost before it has begun.'

Gregory nodded, already thinking of ways to win the favour of Charity. 'And the third?'

'The *enfant perdu*, in the military sense, of course.'

'A lost child?' Gregory waited in silence for an explanation as Leggett sipped his drink.

'Are you familiar with the military concept of a forlorn hope? Those soldiers willing to risk certain death and lead a charge, straight into the enemy cannons?'

'They seek great reward.'

'Weighed against almost certain failure,' Leggett confirmed. 'That describes Hope Strickland. She is a girl with a plan. A rather stupid plan, in my opinion. But it is hers and she cannot be dissuaded.'

'And what would that be?'

'She means to wed the new Earl as soon as the fellow's shoes touch British soil. She thinks his marrying into the family will soften the blow of learning that the Dowager has been pinching his property.'

'Such a connection would be expedient,' Gregory said.

'It would save us the trouble of finding a husband for Charity,' Leggett agreed. 'She has spurned Faith's offer to share our home and refuses to put herself in the way of gentlemen who might court her. But if Hope snags the Earl, Charity could remain in the Comstock Manor library as though nothing had changed.'

It sounded almost like he was describing a piece of furniture that was valuable, but too heavy to move.

'All the same,' Leggett continued, 'a man should have some say in choosing his own wife.'

'And you know nothing about him,' Gregory added. 'He might already be married.'

Leggett nodded. 'Or he might be too young to marry. Or old and without the vigour for it. Also, he will have to be even-tempered enough to forgive the pilfering and inclined to care more for family than the money that this new title is bringing him.'

'He might not be the sort of man a gently bred girl should marry at all,' Gregory said.

'He could be a drooling idiot, for all we know: a villain, a cad, a deviant or a toss pot. I cannot let Hope marry into misery just to maintain the status quo for her little sister.' Now, Leggett had the worried look that so many of Gregory's clients got when faced with an insolvable problem.

'Women get ideas,' Gregory said in his most reassuring tone. 'Especially when they are thinking of the family and not themselves.'

'My wife was guilty of similar foolishness. When I discovered her, she was about to marry for money over love.' Leggett smiled. 'I managed to set that to rights. But I cannot marry all of them to save them from themselves.' Then he looked at Gregory in a way that hinted that the finding of lost objects would not be the hardest part of his job.

'You do not think that I...' Gregory paused. 'You do not expect me to find them husbands.' He prided himself on his ability to rise to a challenge, but matchmaking was not within his purview.

'Lord, no. We are all agreed that Charity is a lost cause. But Hope is more than pretty enough and will have no trouble finding a husband if she can be persuaded to look for one. I do not want the Season to slip away, or offers to be refused, as she waits like a princess in a tower for a rescue that may never come.'

'You wish me to make enquiries into the heir?'

'Any information would be helpful,' Leggett said. 'Should you find that there is a wife and ten little Stricklands in America, make Hope aware of them so she will abandon her scheme.'

'And if I do not?'

'I would not object to your taking a certain creative licence with the truth,' Leggett said, as optimistic in his own way as Miss Strickland was in hers.

'You wish me to lie to her?' Gregory put it plainly. Though he was not a gentleman by birth, he held his honour as dear, often more dearly than the men who hired him did. If he was to break his word with lies, he had no intention of hiding those untruths under elegant euphemisms like *creative licence*.

Leggett sighed. 'I merely want her to set her sights on the men right in front of her. Do what is necessary to persuade her. I will leave the details of it to you.'

'Thank you.' That left him plenty of room to manoeuvre before resorting to falsehood.

'And you will have ample opportunity to come up with something, since you will be forced to work directly with her. It is Miss Hope Strickland who holds the list of items you must retrieve.' Now Leggett was smiling in satisfaction as if he had made the matter easier and not more complicated.

Gregory began cautiously, not wanting to contradict the man trying to hire him. 'In my experience, the less the family is involved with these matters, the quicker they are handled.'

'I did not claim it would be easy,' Leggett reminded him. And there was that smug smile again, as if it gave him pleasure to see another man suffer what he had endured at the delicate hands of the Strickland sisters and their dotty grandmother. 'I will give you double your usual fee, since, if I am honest, I have brought you two problems, not one.'

More money on the table before he'd even opened his mouth to ask for it. Gregory already knew he could find the missing heirlooms. How hard could it be to prevent a marriage that was unlikely to occur, even without his intervention?

He looked at Leggett's smile and hesitated a moment longer.

'Triple, then. I am eager to depart for the

Continent and wish to be sure that the matter will be settled to my satisfaction.'

The offer was too good to refuse, even if he'd wanted to. 'Consider it done.'

'Thank you. Miss Hope Strickland, Miss Charity and the Dowager are in London for the Season at the Comstock town house in Harley Street. I will tell them to expect your visit.'

'Very good.' There was likely to be nothing good about it. Other than the pay, of course. That was enough to reinforce the smile Gregory gave his new employer.

'And I trust this matter will stay between us?' Leggett said, in the slightly embarrassed tone of someone not used to admitting he had difficulties, much less asking for help with them.

'I shall be the soul of discretion,' Gregory replied. When one made one's living mopping up after the gentry, keeping secrets was part of the job description.

Chapter Two

'Good evening, my lord.' Hope Strickland stood in front of a mirror in the hall of the Comstock town house, examining her smile for traces of insincerity before deciding that it was as near to perfect as she could manage.

Then, she curtsied, analysing the results. She was not inexperienced with the niceties due a peer, but that did not mean she should not practise. First impressions were the most important ones. There could be no flaw in hers.

Not that it was likely to matter. The odds of success were almost nil. But if there was any chance at all to impress the next Earl of Comstock, she meant to try.

Now that Faith had married, Hope was left as oldest. It was her job to carry on as best she could and take care of the family that remained. It was clear, from their scattershot behaviour, that Charity and Grandmama needed all the help they could get.

She dipped again. The bend in her knees was not quite deep enough and her eyes could not seem to hold the fine line between deference and flirtation.

'Are you still at that?' Charity was standing in the doorway, arms folded in disapproval.

'It pays to be prepared,' Hope replied, straightening the curl on the left side of her face that could never seem to follow its mates into a proper coiffure.

'Prepared to bow and scrape for the stranger coming to take our house out from under us?' Charity said.

Hope bit back the urge to announce that it was her sister who needed to mind her manners. Instead, she said, 'It is his house. We are but guests in it.'

'Family, you mean,' Charity responded.

'It would be nice to think so.' Hope turned away from the mirror to face Charity. 'I prefer to take a more realistic view of the situation. Though we share a surname, he has never met us before. He will not think of us as family unless we work hard to make him do so. When he arrives, we should greet him with warm welcomes and friendly smiles.'

'You don't wish to befriend him. You want to marry him. What are your plans if that does not happen? If you mean to be prepared, it should be against all eventualities.' Charity was far too logical for her own good. But that was no surprise. It had always been her nature to find the weakness in any plan and jab mercilessly at it until her opponent relented.

'If the Earl is not impressed with me, we shall have to make decent matches while we are in town. Then we will set up our own households and not concern ourselves with him or his property.' She put a subtle emphasis on the word *we,* hoping that her sister would acknowledge the seriousness of the situation and do her share to fix it. Hope had no real fear of failure for herself. But they had always known that things would not be as easy for Charity. And as she usually did, Charity was making matters worse with her refusal to even look for a husband.

'We must also thank Mr Leggett for his generosity in making a Season possible,' Hope added. She touched her skirt to remind her sister of the elegant wardrobes they'd purchased since coming to town. Before their sister had married, it had felt as if they'd been trimming, re-trimming and altering the same tired gowns for ages. But now, everything in their cupboards was fresh and new.

But you could not tell it from looking at Charity, who was wearing a gown that was two years old and could best be described as serviceable. It had done well enough for hiding in the manor library, but it was totally wrong for London. Her sister had noticed her silent criticism and responded, 'There will be time for me to play dress up later. Right now, I have other plans.'

Hope gave her a firm but encouraging smile. 'Of course you do. But it will be rather hard to carry them out while rusticating in the country.'

'For you, perhaps. I was doing quite well right where I was. The sooner you allow me to return to Berkshire the easier it will be on all of us.' While Hope had jumped at the chance to come to town, Charity had done nothing but complain since the moment they'd arrived.

'You speak of my need for alternate plans,' Hope said, smiling to hide her frustration. 'Do you have any of your own? When the Earl arrives, you cannot simply dig in your heels and refuse to vacate the manor. If he asks you to go, you will have to leave.'

Charity smiled. 'I do not need a second plan. The first one is near to fruition and I will be long gone before he ever sets foot in the house. If you would only allow me to return to the country…'

And there it was, again. The solution her little sister was continually hinting at, but refused to reveal. It did not sound as though she meant to reason with the new owner—as if there was a man on the planet who wished to be reasoned with by a girl just out of the schoolroom. But if not that, then what could it be? 'This plan of yours…' Hope hinted. 'I assume it does not include marriage? Because to achieve that, you might consider accepting some of the invitations you receive.'

Then, a worrisome thought struck her. 'Promise me you do not mean to dishonour yourself. We are not as desperate for money as all that.'

Charity laughed harshly. 'My dear sister, you may lie to yourself about your own future, but please do not lie about mine. She stepped forward and took Hope by the shoulders, turning her so they stood reflected, side by side in the mirror. 'No man will have me for a mistress. I am not pretty enough. I fully intend to marry, when the time is right. But it will take more than a new gown and a perfect curtsy for me to catch a husband. I will need a dowry.' She reached up and adjusted her spectacles, as if assessing her own appearance. 'A substantial one, I should think. It will take more money than average to compensate for both appearance and manner.'

'Do not say that about yourself,' Hope said hurriedly. But it was true. It was one thing to be a plain girl and quite another to be an intelligent one who could not manage to keep her opinions to herself. 'I am sure, once the Earl comes…'

'You will marry him, and he will look kindly on your beloved but eccentric, spinster sister?' Charity patted her shoulder. 'You are normally a very sensible girl, Hope. That is why it pains me to see you delude yourself.'

'I just want to see you happy,' Hope said. It was not as much a want as a responsibility. Now that Faith was gone, someone had to look out for the family and neither Charity nor Grandmama had the sense to take charge.

'I am happy,' Charity said softly. 'It may surprise you to hear it, but it is true. Do not concern yourself with my future. Think of your own. I hear Grandmother has got vouchers for Almack's. You must go and dance every dance, even without the presence of the Earl.'

'Of course,' Hope said, then gave her sister a pointed look. 'And you will come with me.'

'Perhaps,' Charity agreed, oblivious to the order she had been given. Then she kissed Hope on the cheek and turned to go up the stairs to her room. 'If I am not busy with something more important.'

Hope sighed. It was better than a flat refusal. Knowing Charity, by Wednesday there would be some excuse that would prevent her from coming out with them. But it did not matter. Just as her sister had suggested, Hope would go and dance until her feet ached. She would be as charming as she possibly could and see to it that every gentleman in London had met and been dazzled by Miss Strickland.

There was no point in being a wallflower. The new Earl of Comstock could have his pick of any girl in England. He would not look twice at a girl who was not courted by others.

She turned back to the mirror, and flashed a smile that would blind a duke at twenty paces. Then, the curtsy. 'Good evening, my lord.' This time, she dipped deeper and felt an embarrassing tremble in her front knee. She was nearly one and twenty, but hardly infirm. She could do better. She must do better.

She tried again. 'Good evening, my lord.'

'I should think good morning would be more appropriate. It is not yet eleven.'

She stumbled at the sound of a voice behind her and raised her eyes to see the reflection of the stranger who had entered the room as she practised.

It was he.

It had to be. Who else but the Earl of Comstock would be wandering around the house unintroduced, as if he owned it? In a sense, he did.

'And I have no title.'

'As of yet,' she said. There was no longer a need to practise her smile. When she looked at him, it came naturally. Who would not be happy in the presence of such a handsome man? Though she had never been one to dote on the male form, his was perfectly proportioned, neither too tall nor too short, with slim hips and broad shoulders on which rested the head of a Roman God. His blond hair was cut *à la* Brutus, curling faintly at the fringe that framed a noble brow, unmarked by signs of worry. His grey eyes were intelligent, his smile sympathetic.

Praise God, she had been delivered just the man she'd prayed would come: young, handsome and, judging by the twinkle that shone in those beautiful eyes as he looked at her, single. But not for long, if she had her way.

He tilted his head. 'You are correct. I have no title, as of yet. Nor am I likely to get one. But they are sometimes awarded to men whose service merits them and I am not yet thirty. With time and effort, anything is possible, Miss Strickland.'

She steadied herself from the shock and turned to face him with as much grace as possible, struggling to maintain the expression she'd been practising in the mirror. 'Then you are not my cousin from America?'

'The future Earl of Comstock?' His smile softened. 'Unfortunately, no.' He bowed from the waist. 'Gregory Drake, at your service,

Miss Strickland. I was told you'd be expecting me.'

She could feel her smile faltering and struggled against the impolite response, *who?*

More importantly, *how?* She glanced to the front door which had not opened to admit anyone, much less this interloper. Then, she made an effort to compose herself. 'I fear you were incorrectly informed. I was not told there would be a guest this morning. You have caught me unprepared.'

He followed her eyes, read the meaning and gave a deferential dip of his head. 'I beg your pardon, Miss Strickland. I was retained by your brother-in-law to help with certain difficulties your family is experiencing. Since the matter is one that requires discretion, I entered through the rear to avoid calling attention.'

'The tradesman's entrance.' Of course he had. If Mr Leggett had hired him, why should he not begin there?

He nodded, solemnly.

A torrent of unladylike words filled her mind about trumped-up nobodies with delusions of a grand future who had the gall to tease her with them. And worse yet, who had the nerve to look like the answer to a maiden's prayers. He had no right to be so handsome, yet so inappropriate.

Then, the rant changed to encompass her sister's husband, who had hired this…this…person. She ended with a scold for Grandmama, who probably knew the whole story and had neglected to tell her any of it, just as she had with the difficulties surrounding an audit. The Dowager probably thought it amusing to throw the two of them together so Hope might make a fool of herself.

When she was sure that her actual words would leave her mouth with a minimum of bile, she said, 'So Mr Leggett has sent you to save us from ourselves.'

Her control was not perfect. She still sounded ungrateful, but she had a right to be angry. She had been behaving like an idiot when he'd entered. It likely confirmed what he already thought of the family: that they were a houseful of silly women, incapable of caring for themselves.

Of course, that was what she often thought, when faced with the latest exploit of her sister or her grandmother. She did not deny that they had problems, but how could a stranger possibly understand them the way she did?

She forced another smile. It was not the warm one she was saving for the Earl. The one she gave to Mr Drake was sufficient for solicitors and shopkeepers. 'How much has Mr Leggett told you about our difficulty?'

'Everything, I suspect. You seek the return of certain items before an impending inventory.' If he thought her rude, he did not show it. His manner reflected hers. He was professionally pleasant, but revealed no trace of his true thoughts or feelings.

So, he suspected he knew everything. That proved how little he actually knew. Even Mr Leggett did not know the worst of it for Hope had not wished to ruin Faith's honeymoon with what she had recently discovered. But Mr Drake should at least understand that none of it was Hope's fault. To prove her lack of culpability, she said aloud the words that had been echoing in her mind since she had learned the extent of their troubles. 'Grandmama should not have sold things that did not belong to her. Nor should she have kept our financial difficulties a secret for so long.'

He offered another sympathetic nod. 'But what could you have done, had you known?'

Very little. Faith had been the one in charge

of the family budget and her decisions had seemed sensible enough. Economies had been taken in diet and dress. Rooms had been shut and staff had been released. How much less would they have had without Grandmama's judicious thefts refilling the accounts?

The fact that there had been no other solution did not make her feel any better, now that reckoning had arrived. 'The past does not matter. It is the future that I am worried about. There will be a scandal, if the truth comes out.'

'I am here to see that it never does,' he said. 'I have helped more than a few families with similar problems. Taking desperate measures when there is a shortage of funds is not at all unusual.'

'I assume Mr Leggett means to buy back the lost items?' It was a generous plan from a man who had no idea the depth of the problem.

'He said you had a list.'

'After a fashion,' she said, giving nothing away. By the look on Mr Drake's face, he expected her to turn over the details of her family's darkest secrets without as much as a by your leave. She had no reason to trust this stranger who appeared out of nowhere with far too much information and no introduction, verbal or written. For all she knew, he was an agent of the new Earl and they were already discovered.

He gave another encouraging smile. 'If you share it with me, then I will go about my business and leave you to yours. The matter will be settled without another thought from you.'

She could not help a derisive snort. It would serve him right if she told him the truth and then sent him on his way with no other help. 'Very well, then.' She turned from him and walked down the hall to the morning room. He could follow or not. It did not really matter.

She heard the measured steps of his boots follow down the corridor and into the room. When she withdrew the crumpled paper from the little writing desk in the corner, she turned to find him still a respectful few steps behind her. She handed him the list. 'There you go. Settle our troubles, if you still think you can.'

She watched his handsome brow furrow as he read down the column. 'Blue painting. Candlesticks. Third Earl's inkwell.' He glanced up at her, clearly surprised. 'That is all the detail you have? Nothing to tell me if the candlesticks were gold or silver?' The furrows grew even deeper. 'And I cannot make out this line at all.'

'Neither can I,' she said, trying to contain the malicious glee as he was brought into her suffering. 'My grandmother is a woman of many words, but we can seldom get the ones we need out of her. It took some effort to get this much detail, for she kept no records of the things she sold and the places she took them. And I am quite certain there are items missing from this account.' Only one of them had any significance. But it was not a story she wished to tell, just yet. 'I will question her further, but I do not know how much more she will admit.'

'It is fortunate that dealers keep better records than their clients,' he said. 'It might take some persuading for them to give the information up. There are laws against dealing in entailed merchandise.'

'I am well aware of the fact.' Her grandmother was as guilty or more so than the people she'd bartered with. They might be receivers of stolen goods, but she was the actual thief.

'But if they do not remember her?' The look

on his face changed to resignation. 'Would you recognise these items, if you saw them again?'

'Most of them, I think,' she said. 'I have lived in the house since I was ten. They should at least be familiar, should I find them in a shop window.'

He sighed. 'Then it would be best if you come with me, to retrieve them.'

'You are suggesting that I accompany a strange man to unseemly parts of London to retrieve stolen goods.'

'I am not a stranger, as such,' he reminded her. His smile returned, though it was somewhat the worse for wear. 'I was sent by your brother-in-law to help you.'

'I have only your word for that,' she replied.

'How else would I know of your problems, if not for him?'

'You might have guessed them.' More likely, it was just as he said. He had been sent to help. But for some reason, his good looks and perfect manners annoyed her. It gave her a dark and unladylike pleasure to see him struggle.

His composure slipped for only a moment. Then he dug a hand into his coat pocket and came out with a paper. He held it out to her. 'If it is not as I say, how do you suppose I came by this?'

It was a letter of credit, signed by Mr Leggett, promising to honour any and all bills without question. The sight of it left her light-headed. He could not know what he was promising. Since Faith and her husband had already left for their honeymoon, it was too late to tell him.

He mistook the reason for her silence and said, 'If it helps, think of me as a servant who will be accompanying you as you set matters right. I will be there to assure your safety, handle the transactions and carry the packages.'

It did not help at all. The idea of him walking a pace behind her like some liveried footman was an abomination. He was too well spoken for a servant and not stern enough for a schoolmaster. If she stretched her imagination to the breaking point, she could see him as a solicitor, but there was a sparkle in his eye better suited to a criminal than a man of law. And no vicar would have that knowing smile.

He was simply too handsome to be going about town with. Should she be seen with him there would be gossip that had nothing to do with the Stricklands' financial troubles. And while it was quite all right for the new Earl to see her as sought after, she could not have him thinking that she was being actively courted by Gregory Drake.

'If you fear for your reputation, remember that it will be equally damaged if news of the missing items becomes public.'

'Unless the new Earl can be persuaded to compassionate silence,' she said, wishing she could go back to her practising and pretend this meeting had never occurred.

Mr Drake tucked his letter back into his coat, along with her incomplete list. 'What do you know of your grandfather's heir, thus far?'

It was an annoying question, since the answer was obvious. They'd had no contact with the man, other than the request for an audit of the entail to be completed before his arrival, and that had come through a solicitor. It did not bode well. But she put on a false smile to appease her interrogator. 'I know that he is family and familial bonds are strong. I am sure Mr Strickland will understand the difficulties faced by women who are forced to fend for themselves.'

'We must hope so, for I doubt he has any special affection for this country,' Mr Drake said, pulling another piece of paper from his opposite pocket. 'Mr Leggett has also hired me to find what I could about the gentleman you are expecting.' He scanned his notes. 'It appears that his grandfather fought bravely in their revolution against this country. More recently, Mr Strickland's elder brother, Edward, was impressed into the British Navy. Miles Strickland became heir upon Edward's untimely death in battle.'

This was what came of optimism. Hope had allowed herself to believe, just once, that with a little effort on her part, things might turn out for the best. And this was how the Lord rewarded her. She swallowed her nerves. 'If our country has treated him so unfairly, perhaps he will refuse the title and remain in America.'

'It is too late to hope for that, I think,' Mr Drake announced. 'Even now, the schooner *Mary Beth* is on its way from Philadelphia to Bristol. If he booked passage on it, as he planned, he may arrive at any time.'

'We are not at fault for a war on the other side of the world, or the doings of the Royal

Navy,' Hope said, feeling her vision of the future crumbling like a sandcastle at high tide.

'But there is still the matter of the missing entail,' Mr Drake replied, speaking slowly, as if to a child. 'It is best that we make sure he has no other reasons to be unhappy with you. Give me a day to examine your list in detail. If it is convenient, I will call for you tomorrow at ten and we will begin the process of making things right.'

She wanted to argue that it was not convenient at all. He could take the list and go to perdition for all she cared. They were doomed. All doomed. What good would it do her to start a search that she was sure they could never finish?

But Mr Leggett must have chosen this fellow for his skills in retrieval. Perhaps he could find a way to make things marginally better. If he needed her help, then surely her help was required. The sooner it was begun, the sooner it would be over. And she could not depend on rough winter crossings to delay the Earl indefinitely. The house needed to be in something approaching order when he arrived at it. She forced another smile for Mr Drake. 'If this is to be settled, I do not see that I have any choice in the matter. I will accompany you as long as certain conditions are met.'

'And they are?' he said, with an expectant tip of his head.

'For the sake of modesty, I will remain veiled in your presence. We will speak no more than is necessary and under no circumstances will you call me by name while in the presence of others.'

If he was insulted there was no sign of it. His smile was as distant and unwavering as ever. 'Of course, Miss Strickland.'

'Then I will expect you at ten o'clock tomorrow.'

'Until then.' He offered a bow worthy of a true gentleman, then spoiled it by turning towards the back of the house.

She sighed. 'You are standing next to a door, Mr Drake. Please, use it.'

'As you wish, Miss Strickland. He turned and let himself out of the front door and into the street.

Hope moved to the window and watched him walk down Harley Street, sure she could not truly breathe until he was out of sight. Mr Leggett meant well, as did Mr Drake. Even if it did not make things better, their interference

could not possibly make things worse. But had
it been necessary to tell her about the Earl of
Comstock's antipathy for England? It was almost as if Mr Drake took as much pleasure in
seeing her disappointment as she had in his.

'My, what a charming fellow.' Grandmother
stood behind her, looking out the window at
their departing visitor.

'He was not charming,' Hope said, wondering if her grandmother had formed her opinion based on the way the man's coat hugged
his shoulders as he walked. 'And how would
you know, either way? You did not speak to
him, did you?'

Grandmother peered past her at the retreating figure. 'Only briefly, when he arrived.
He is the fellow James hired to help us with
the entail.'

'You knew.' Hope could not help her shrill
tone at the discovery that, once again, she had
been denied important information and left
in an awkward situation to fend for herself.

'Did I forget to mention it?' She looked
at Hope with the widened eyes of one who
thought that age and good intentions made up
for outright lies. 'I did not want to trouble you.
But when he arrived looking so young and

handsome, I assumed the two of you would not want an old chaperon spoiling a perfectly lovely chat.'

Just as she had suspected. 'You sent a strange man to speak to me without as much as a footman to explain.' She probably assumed that if she threw the two of them together they would stick like lodestones, just as Faith and James had. 'I cannot solve our problems by marrying the first person who walks through the door, you know.'

Her normally cheerful grandmother arched a sceptical eyebrow. 'You are a fine one to say such a thing. That is your plan, is it not? To marry the new Earl?'

'That is entirely different,' Hope replied. At least she knew the Earl's family. Lord only knew what sort of dubious pedigree Mr Drake might have.

'It is not the worst idea,' the Dowager admitted. 'But as I tried to explain to your sister Faith, choosing a husband for financial expediency is never as satisfying as a union based on mutual affection.' She stared down the street in the direction Mr Drake had disappeared. 'Or, at least, temporary passion. That fellow was quite handsome, I thought.'

It was annoyingly true. His hair was the colour of winter wheat and, though she'd often thought grey eyes seemed cold, his were warm and inquisitive, especially when paired with that slightly sardonic smile. 'I did not notice his looks,' she lied.

'Are you ill?' Her grandmother reached out to touch her forehead.

Hope shook off the hand. 'Merely circumspect. My parents would have thought it most unchristian of me to evaluate a man on appearance alone.'

The older woman gave a disapproving tut. 'When we encouraged your father to read for the church, we had no idea he would take the whole thing so seriously.'

Both her parents had been more than serious on the subject of morality. They'd been paragons of it, and died together, nursing their village through an epidemic. Then, Hope and her sisters had come to live with their grandparents and a whole new and comparatively decadent world had been opened to them. 'They would have wanted me to marry sensibly,' Hope replied. 'There is nothing sensible about Mr Drake.'

'A flirtation, then,' her grandmother suggested, with no thought at all to Hope's reputation. But then, as she frequently reminded them all, things had been different when she was a girl.

'Young ladies do not engage in flirtations,' Hope reminded her. They especially did not do it with employees of their families and she did not think Mr Drake was helping them out of the goodness of his heart.

'I am not suggesting that you dishonour yourself,' the Dowager added with a flutter of her lashes. 'But it would not hurt you to smile when you see a handsome man. It would not ruin you to laugh with him. The world will not end if you let him steal a kiss.'

'Actually, it might,' Hope said. 'Suppose someone learned of it? I would be shunned from polite society and Mr Drake would not be welcome in the homes of the men who employ him.'

The Dowager sighed. 'Young people nowadays have no spirit at all.'

'Gentlemen do not marry girls who have too much spirit,' Hope replied.

'All the more reason *not* to marry a gentleman,' she supplied. 'Of course, it is possible that the new Earl will not be one. He is American, after all. Lord knows what barbaric habits he has developed.'

'He is probably married,' Hope said, glumly. It would be just her luck if he turned out to be a married man who hated the English.

'Then, perhaps you should look elsewhere. As I reminded you before, Mr Drake is a very handsome man.'

Hope offered a weak smile in response. At times like this, she was never sure if her grandmother was joking, addled by age or simply lost to all propriety. But she had lived with the Dowager far too long to be surprised.

'Mr Drake has no interest in me, beyond the task set for him by Mr Leggett. There will be no lingering glances, no stolen kisses and definitely no marriage. We will find what missing items we can, he will collect his payment and that will be the end of it.'

'If you say so, my dear.' The Dowager shook her head in disappointment. 'But in my opinion, you are wasting an opportunity.'

'I certainly hope so,' Hope replied with an adamant nod of her head.

Chapter Three

So far, the Strickland family was everything Leggett had promised they would be: intelligent, maddening and beautiful. Though of those attributes, the best the Dowager Countess could seem to manage was two out of three.

Judging by her granddaughter, she had been stunning thirty-odd years ago, and was still a handsome woman. But from the dearth of information she'd provided about the problems she'd caused, it was clear the Earl had not married her for her mind. When Gregory had tried to question her upon arriving at the town house, she had deliberately changed the subject, wanting to know more about him than he had cared to share while revealing nothing at all about the shops she had frequented or the things she'd sold to them.

Then, there was Miss Hope Strickland, who was currently sitting beside him in a rented carriage on their way to a pawnshop. She was simmering like a soup kettle with the desire to finish her part in the search as quickly as possible so she might never lay eyes on him again.

And a very pretty kettle of soup she was. Chestnut hair, large brown eyes and a pert nose accented the sort of soft, curvy body a man longed to hold. But the set of her beautiful shoulders and the straight line of her eminently kissable lips had assured him of the unlikelihood that anything would happen between them. She was the granddaughter of an earl and had heard the common 'Mister' before his name and dismissed him out of hand.

Likewise, he had noted her grandfather's rank before even meeting her and had come to the same conclusion. He was not the sort of fellow who dallied with female clients, especially when there were titles involved. When one was a living example of what might happen when such niceties were ignored, one did not take them lightly.

At the moment, Miss Hope sat beside him silent, cloaked and veiled, as if his very presence brought a risk of contagion. Her desire for anonymity made perfect sense. But there was something annoying in the way she had demanded it, as if she had not trusted him to protect her unless ordered to do so. It left him with the urge to strip off one of her gloves and touch her bare hand, just to see if she melted from upper-class perfection to a wailing puddle of mediocrity. Or at least tug on the curl that had been bouncing at the side of her face yesterday. This morning, it had been held in place by not just one but two hair pins, as if she was punishing it for being unruly.

Hope Strickland was the sort of woman who liked both people and things to be orderly, proper and predictable. He would likely be a great disappointment to her. Hopefully, they could manage to put their differences aside while working together. Until the matter of the entail was settled, they would be near to inseparable.

He glanced towards her and away again, hoping she had not noticed his interest. It felt as if, somewhere deep inside his head, an alarm bell was ringing. They should not be alone together. It was dangerous to her reputation and to his…

Something.

He wasn't sure exactly why, but he knew in his bones that he shouldn't be alone with her and it had nothing to do with society's expectations of virtuous young ladies. He had no worries about self-control, either hers or his own. But the silence in the cab was wearing on his nerves. It made him want to converse, even though she had made it quite clear she did not want to speak to him.

He should never have requested her help. It was not as if he had to find the exact items again. He merely needed a good approximation. The American Stricklands had not spent the long years away pining for the candlesticks they meant to retrieve today. One set would be much like another to the new Earl, as long as he did not note an absence of light in the dining room.

But what the devil did the Dowager mean by an 'oddment'? It was the only word he had deciphered in the line of scribbling near the bottom of the list. And how was he to decide which 'blue painting' was the correct one? Only a member of the family could guide him through the inadequate descriptions provided to him and Miss Hope Strickland was the only one willing to help.

But since she had done so begrudgingly, he had a perverse desire to see her discommoded. That was why he had chosen the worst shop on the list as their first stop. There would be almost no chance at success for it traded in the saddest of merchandise, not the sort of things likely to be found in one of England's greatest houses. While he knew that there were better hunting grounds ahead, she would leave the shop coated in the miasma of despair that seemed to hang about the financial misfortune of others.

The carriage stopped in front of a plain door in St Giles, marked with the traditional three balls that indicated its business. He exited, offering a hand to Miss Strickland to help her to the street, while keeping a wary eye out for the cutpurses and beggars that would appear to harass the gentry.

To his surprise, she did not shrink back in terror at the riff-raff that surrounded them. But neither did she offer thanks for his assistance. Instead, she sailed imperiously past him to stand expectantly at the door, waiting for him to open it.

It was only common courtesy that he do so, but for some reason, it rankled. All the same, he opened and she passed through. And at last he was rewarded with the response he'd expected, the utter confusion of a gently bred lady who had never before shopped for someone else's cast-offs.

She paused in the entryway as if afraid to go further. He could tell by the subtle shifting of her bonnet that her eyes were darting around the room, stunned to immobility by the cases of brass buttons and mismatched earbobs, and racks upon racks of shabby coats and fashionless gowns.

He shut the door and stepped past her. A quick scan of the room proved that none of the finer items would be found here, but he had no intention of leaving without making an enquiry, lest Miss Strickland realise he'd only come here to torture her. He rang the bell on the counter to summon the proprietor.

The man who stepped out from behind the curtained back room was every bit as fearsome as he'd hoped, a gaunt scarecrow of a fellow with one eye that did not seem to want to follow the other. It gave the impression that he could watch both his customers at the same time. At the sight of him, the girl who had been so quick to treat Gregory as her lackey now faded one step behind him, trying to disappear into his shadow.

It made him smile more broadly than he might have as he greeted the pawnbroker. 'Good morning, my fine fellow. I am seeking candlesticks. Not just any candlesticks, mind you. I want the sort the posh types pawn when they can't pay their gambling debts.'

The man answered with a nod and a toothless grin, then pointed wordlessly into the corner at a small display of plate.

Gregory glanced at it for only a moment, before choosing the gaudiest pair and walking back towards the counter. He felt a sharp tug on his sleeve and looked back at Miss Strickland.

'Those are not ours,' she whispered.

'I thought you could not describe what we were looking for,' he countered.

'I cannot. But I am sure that I have never seen those in my life.'

'Neither has Miles Strickland. He has never seen England, much less these candlesticks.'

'That does not make them right,' she countered. 'Ignorance is no substitute for truth.'

Perhaps not. But in Gregory's opinion, it made for a pretty fine excuse and had worked well in the past. 'It is not as if we will be lying to him. He will expect to find candlesticks and we are leaving him some. He will never know the difference.'

'But I will,' she said.

Hadn't Leggett said something about the sisters being the daughters of a vicar? If so, their ingrained morality was proving deeply inconvenient. 'Your sister's husband is not paying me enough to turn the town upside down for things that are likely lost for ever.'

'If all that was needed was to grab the first things that came to hand, I could have done it myself.' Noting the wary way she had watched the proprietor, he doubted that was the case. But she had no trouble standing up to Gregory, for he saw a faint flash of irritation in the brown eyes glittering behind her veil. 'I do not know what he is paying you, but I am sure Mr Leggett did not hire you to do the job halfway. If the funds were insufficient, you should have negotiated for more when he hired you.'

For a sheltered young lady she was surprisingly perceptive. She was annoying as well. But his fee had been tripled to account for that.

He gave her a subservient smile. 'Very well, then. I shall try harder.'

He turned back to the shopkeeper. 'You have a very small collection for an item that is one of the first to be sold, when the gentry's pockets are to let. Are there any others in the shop?'

The man favoured them with his wall-eyed gaze for a moment and Gregory set a coin on the counter. 'For the inconvenience of opening your stockroom to us, good sir.'

The man pocketed the coin and stepped back, pulling the curtain to the side to let them pass.

The little room at the back of the shop was cluttered, as he expected it to be, but not without organisation. The shelves were full of more dented bird cages, tarnished tea-kettles and chipped vases than could be sold in a lifetime. Beneath them were an equally large number of chests, full of silver flatware and... Lo and behold, candlesticks.

He threw back the lid and lit a nearby candle to supplement the meagre light streaming from a grimy window on the back wall. Then he gestured Miss Strickland closer. 'Here you are. If the items are to be found in this shop, you are the only one who might tell. Look for yourself.'

He had expected a shudder of distaste and the demand that he sort through the chest and display the contents to her. Instead, all her reservations fell away. She pushed back the veil and dropped to her knees on the floor beside it, digging without hesitation through the pile of dented flambeaus and sconces.

Suddenly, she sighed in surprise and turned to him with a dented pewter stick clutched in her hands. She offered it to him and reached up to push back her bonnet. Then she smoothed her hair out of the way, leaving a streak of tarnish on her soft, white brow. 'Does it match?'

He frowned in confusion and leaned forward to look closer. The decoration she held was designed to imitate a Corinthian column, the top a square of ornate tracery. On her forehead was a small V-shaped scar with a break that matched a gap in the decoration.

'Someone hit you with this?' He hefted the weight of it in his hands and felt the anger rise in his gorge at the brutality of the late Earl, her grandfather.

She nodded. Then, oddly, she smiled. 'My sister, Charity.' Her hand dived back into the chest and pulled out the mate, which was bent at the base. 'In response, I threw this one at her. But I missed and it hit the dining-room wall. There is still a crack in the plaster where it landed.'

He felt momentarily weak as the rage left him again. 'That is good to know. I would hate to think that either of you had a skull thick enough to cause such damage to it.' But if they had, it ought not to have surprised him. Hope Strickland was proving to be the most hard-headed woman he'd ever met. He doubted her sister was any different.

She was still smiling. 'Then, Faith came and pulled both our plaits until we cried. I had forgotten all about that.' She was looking fondly at the candlesticks, as if meeting old friends. She frowned. 'And now, we will have to give them to a complete stranger, just because he shares our name.'

Her dark mood disappeared as quickly as it had come. She looked back up at him, so fresh and unguarded that he felt a lump rising in his throat. 'But I remember this. It is why just any candlestick would not do. Perhaps the new Earl would not know the difference, but it would not be the same to me.'

'I understand.' He stared at the smudge on her forehead in fascination. He wanted to wipe it away, smoothing a finger over that small, white vee in wonder. A flaw should make her uglier, not more fascinating. Was it raised, he wondered, or smooth? A single touch, under the guise of cleaning away the grime, would tell him.

He cleared his mind, cleared his throat and pulled a handkerchief from his pocket, offering it to her. 'You have…' he touched his own forehead '…here.'

She gave him a misty smile and a shrug of embarrassment before wiping away the dirt and returning his linen to him.

He was no less intrigued once it was gone. Perhaps it was her reaction to the injury that drew him to her. He'd been in such childhood scraps himself, but did not remember any of them as fondly as she did hers.

Of course, he'd had no brother to strike him. He did not often think of that, either. But suddenly there was a strange emptiness in him, as if he was hungry, but could not decide for what.

It was probably tea. The single slice of toast he'd had for breakfast had burned away hours ago. He needed sustenance to fill his belly and clear his mind. The sooner they left this store and returned Miss Strickland to her town house, the sooner he could remedy the hunger. He held out one hand for the heirlooms and another to help her to her feet. 'Come. Let us pay for the return of these. Perhaps, tomorrow we can find your painting.'

They went back to the carriage and rode in silence back to Harley Street, where he handed her down to the waiting footman and carried the brown-paper bundle containing the candlesticks into the house for her.

The smugness he felt at today's success did not do him credit. He had been confident of his ability to deliver a satisfactory solution to Leggett's problem. But he had not expected to find a reasonable duplicate on the very first day, much less an actual item. Despite his employer's warnings that the entire family was nothing but trouble, Hope Strickland might actually be the key to completion.

There was still the matter of her plans for the unsuspecting American. But since they had resulted from her lack of confidence that the entail could be made complete, today's success might have loosened her grip on them.

It had been quite gratifying to see the look on her face when they had found the candlesticks. Since he had caught her practising her smiles in a mirror, he'd doubted that any of the ones she'd given him were born of sincerity. In his experience, the ruling class was good at appearing to be things they weren't: kind, friendly and happy, for instance.

But her grin when she'd pulled the family silver out of that chest had been positively impish. The youthful mischief in her expression was a million miles away from the aloof mask she'd worn for the rest of their time together.

When she'd looked up at him, bathing him in an aura of true happiness, he'd had to remind himself that his reward for taking the job was not actually the smile of a beautiful young lady. He was doing this for money.

The proper Miss Strickland had seemed disgusted by the idea when she had talked of his fee. In her world, women might sell themselves to the highest bidder for a loveless marriage without turning a hair, but men were expected to do things for country, gallantry or sport. They never did anything as common as earning a living.

But as she'd talked of her childhood, she had forgotten what he was and looked at him as if he were an equal. Better yet, she had seen him as a man. There had been surprise on her face and perhaps a little awe in his ability to help her so easily. He had been flattered. He was smiling at her now, as he set the package on the dining-room table.

She looked up at him, as she removed her bonnet, and gave a slight toss of her head to free the last strand of her hair from the ribbon. Then, she smiled back at him with a puzzled expression that proved her earlier lapse was forgotten. 'Thank you for your help, Mr Drake. The day was more productive than I expected. But now I must go and change for dinner.'

It took a moment to recognise the reason for her statement. He meant nothing to her. In fact, she seemed a little surprised that it had been necessary to dismiss him. When servants were finished being useful, they were expected to disappear until the next time they were needed.

Instead, he had been standing there like an idiot, as if he thought they had a reason to converse socially. It was the same feeling that had come over him in the carriage and he must gain control of it immediately. He forced a polite nod in response and said, 'Of course, Miss Strickland. If it is convenient, I will return tomorrow and we will try another shop.'

Her already relaxed expression seemed to become even more placid. She gave a contented sigh, secure in the knowledge that they understood each other. 'That will be fine, Mr Drake. And now, if you will excuse me?'

He bowed and she turned and left him to find his own way out.

He stood for a moment, staring after her, annoyed with her and with himself. When contemplating his place in society, he was not normally given to envy or dissatisfaction. By dint of his own effort, he had gained wealth and comfort and was smart enough not to be burdened by the sort of problems that led people to hire him. He was more than happy.

But today that did not feel like enough.

'Mr Drake.'

He jumped at the sound of his name. The girl who had spoken it was staring at him from the doorway. Leggett had said that she was but nineteen years old, yet there was something about the look in her spectacled eyes that made her seem much older. The illusion was encouraged by the rather old-fashioned way she wore her straight brown hair and the utilitarian cut of her gown.

'Miss Charity, I presume,' he said, bowing deeply.

She nodded. 'We have not been introduced. But then, you had not been introduced to my sister when you barged in on her yesterday.'

Apparently, there were no secrets in the Strickland family, especially not as they related to the harassing of strangers. He nodded in acknowledgement. 'Your grandmother led me to believe I was expected.'

She gave him a dubious smile.

He held out his open hands and shrugged. 'I gave her my card and she told me to find your sister in the hall. She assured me that Miss Strickland would know exactly what it was that needed doing. She made no offer of introduction. I assumed none was necessary.'

Miss Charity's expression grew only slightly

less doubtful. 'If I were you, I would be very careful in following when the Dowager is the one in front. She veers wide of the truth when it suits her.'

'Why would it suit her to…?'

'Lie?' The girl finished his question with the same strange, knowing smile. 'Because in recent years, the truth has been quite unpleasant. She prefers to live in the past where things were easier.'

'But what does any of that have to do with me?'

'She would like my sister to be as happy as she was, in her youth. To achieve that, she must find a man for Hope.' Charity paused for a moment. 'Or men. I am unsure how many of the stories she tells are true, but they are always very colourful.'

'I see.' In truth, he did not. 'What does that have to do with me?'

Miss Charity looked over her glasses at him. 'You are male, are you not?'

'Of course. But what…?' And then, the truth came clear. 'You cannot mean—'

'I would not take it personally,' Charity interrupted. 'My sister has been uninclined to search for a husband outside of the one outlandish candidate she waits for. If Grand-mother chose to throw a handsome man into her afternoon without warning, it was more of a call to awaken the senses rather than an actual attempt to mate the pair of you.'

At the clinical way she described it, he could see why Leggett had not hesitated in tripling his fee. 'That is a comfort, I suppose.'

'But you are not here to settle my sister's future,' she said, watching him more closely than he liked. 'How goes the search for the missing entail?'

'I do not anticipate any problems with it.' He kept his tone polite, professional and opaque.

She gave a shake of her head. 'The whole enterprise is unnecessary, of course.'

'You think so?' he said, surprised. Unlike the rest of the family, she seemed unaffected by the impending audit.

She gave a slight nod. 'If my plan comes to fruition, we need not worry about staying in the heir's good graces. But since you have been hired to complete the inventory to satisfy the rest of the family, feel free to grab items at random that fit the bill. What will some

American know if every bell and button in the house is not just as my grandfather left it?'

'I suggested much the same,' he said. 'But your sister requires greater accuracy than that.'

'Hope appreciates order and is no good at dissembling,' Charity replied. 'She refuses to believe that the rest of us can get away with an adjustment of the truth because she knows she cannot.'

'Such honesty is a thing to be prized,' he said. 'You make it sound like weakness of character.'

'You do not have to live with it,' Charity said. 'At least, not yet.'

He stared at her, waiting for clarification, but none was offered. Perhaps she'd intended it as a joke. He had been told she was a rather odd girl.

'And how do you get along with my sister?' she added, which did not help his peace of mind at all.

'She has been most helpful in establishing the provenance of the item we have found. I appreciate her assistance and anticipate no difficulties in our working together.' He gave her what he hoped was his most distant and professional smile.

'I see,' she said in a way that made him want to demand an explanation of exactly what it was she saw. 'I am sure she will say much the same of you.'

'I am glad to know it,' he said, feeling strangely unsettled by the compliment.

'And is the restoration of the entail your only job for our family?' Charity's searching look had returned, prying at his composure as if looking for a crack.

There was no way she could have known the full scope of his mission. 'What would make you think I was here for another reason?'

'Because I know Mr Leggett,' she said. 'Before he met my sister, he was a rake who did not care at all for propriety, much less love. But now?' She clasped her hands and gave a mocking flutter of her eyelashes. 'He wants everyone to be as happy as he is.'

'That is commendable of him,' Gregory responded.

'Forward is what I would call it,' Charity replied. 'He is right to think that Hope should not wait needlessly for the coming of the Earl.

She will find that for herself if we leave her alone.'

'Of course,' he said.

'But it would be just like a man to try subterfuge once he realises reason will not work. A distracting flirtation, for example...'

'What the devil are you implying?' He regretted the curse immediately, but the words had been so blunt that he'd forgotten he was talking to a young lady. 'I was not sent here to take advantage of your sister.'

'You are a problem solver, are you not, Mr Drake? Why would you not think of the most direct solution?'

'Because I am a gentleman,' he said. And because he knew from experience just what ruin such a thing might cause.

She touched a finger to her chin. 'You claim to be a gentleman. But I can find nothing of your past, or your parentage.'

'If it does not matter to Mr Leggett, why should it matter to you?'

'Because he does not know this family as well as I do,' Charity replied. 'And because, if I am honest, he is not as intelligent as I am. If he had thought through the implications of leaving a stranger to ferry his sister-in-law around London, you'd have already had this conversation with him.'

Gregory had not got as far in life as he had without remaining calm when faced with bigoted questions from the gentry. Normally, he would have spoken of his extensive résumé and presented references from other men of stature who had been satisfied with his performance.

But today, it did not seem to be enough. Only the whole truth would do. 'You could find nothing of my parentage because I do not know it myself. I have been told that my mother was from a good family, but died in childbirth. My father was less so. He seduced her, then abandoned her to her fate. When she died, her family was faced with the problem of an infant whose very existence was a blot on the family honour and the good name of a lost and presumably beloved daughter. They provided for my care and education anonymously, but have never shown an interest in the child I was or the man I have become.'

'I see,' said Miss Charity.

Her assessment annoyed him. 'If you truly do, then you will know that your sister's reputation is perfectly safe with me. Since I cannot prove my honour with a pedigree, I have done it with my behaviour. I have no intention of being the man my father was and leaving a lover dead or disgraced, or a son abandoned to the care of strangers and left to field such questions as the ones you are asking me.' He stared back at her with the same unflinching intensity she had been using on him.

It did not seem to bother her in the least. At last, she sighed in what he hoped was satisfaction. 'Very well, then. You are honourable by choice. That is probably a better reason than those who claim their good name is enough to swear on. My apologies for pressing you to reveal so much of your past. But despite what the family sometimes thinks, I do love my sisters and will not stand by and let them be hurt.'

He answered with a respectful nod.

'And no matter what Mr Leggett may have asked of you, do not interfere too strenuously in Hope's future. It will sort itself once I make her aware of certain facts.'

He gave no response to this at all. Since she was not his employer, what she wanted did not signify.

She pushed her spectacles up her nose,

which seemed to magnify her already large hazel eyes, and fixed him with a gaze that would have been quelling had it come from a man. 'And most important of all, you must not meddle in my affairs, no matter what my sister may wish of you. Keep Hope occupied with restoring the entail. Come to me when you reach the inevitable impasse and I will help you. But until then, do not bother me with it, for I am occupied with more important matters.'

'And what are these matters, Miss Charity?' he said and followed it with his most winning smile.

She touched the side of her nose and winked. 'All in good time, Mr Drake. But I assure you, they have nothing to do with husband-hunting at Almack's.' She glanced at the door. 'Do not let me keep you from your own business.'

And thus, he was dismissed for the second time that day. He bowed to her, as he had to her sister. 'Nor do I wish to keep you from yours, whatever it may be. Good day, Miss Charity.'

'Until tomorrow, Mr Drake.'

Chapter Four

As she waited for Mr Drake's return the next morning, Hope paused to admire the candlesticks which had been polished and displayed on the dining-room sideboard. They belonged in the manor, not in London. But this would have to do until she could arrange for them to be transported.

'So, you actually found something.' Charity stood in the doorway, arms folded across her chest. 'When I heard of your plans to go treasure hunting, I assumed Mr Leggett was wasting his money.'

'On the contrary,' Hope said, running an idle finger along the length of the pewter. 'Mr Drake is very diligent. I have the utmost confidence in him.'

'Grandmother said you did not like him,' Charity said.

'I do not claim to,' Hope answered. 'But I do like these candlesticks. It is nice to see them back in the family.'

'And it was very nice of Mr Leggett to find such a handsome man to retrieve them,' Charity said with a sly smile.

'I had not noticed,' Hope lied.

'Then you are either blind or deliberately obtuse,' Charity said.

'Hmm,' said Hope, turning to the window to watch for the arrival of his coach.

'Of course, he is little better than a servant,' Charity added.

'It is unworthy of you to say such a thing,' Hope said. 'Our own father was a servant to the Lord and Mother was the daughter of Comstock's man of business. If Papa did not have a problem...' She turned back to continue the lecture and saw Charity grinning at her agitation. 'You were baiting me.'

Charity shrugged. 'I just wanted to see if you remembered our origins. Mr Drake thinks you terribly proud.'

'When did you speak to Mr Drake?' More importantly, why had they been discussing her? And had he really formed such a poor opinion of her in only two meetings?

'I might have run into him as he left yesterday morning,' Charity answered.

'You mean you were lurking in the hall, waiting to catch a glimpse of him,' Hope replied. 'You are too young for him, if that is your line of thinking.' Her little sister had shown no real interest in men thus far, which made her sudden curiosity about Mr Drake all the more alarming.

'I am nineteen,' Charity replied. 'Some would say I am just the right age for marriage and at nearly twenty-one you are dangerously near to becoming a spinster.'

'You are still not right for Mr Drake,' Hope said, exasperated. Then she added, 'We do not even know if he is married.'

'Do you wish for me to ask him?'

'Certainly not.' Sometimes, it was convenient to have such a nosy sister, who would satisfy her curiosity without Hope having to admit she had ever wondered. 'It is not our concern whether or not he has a wife.' She sounded as disapproving as she was able, knowing that Charity could rarely resist the forbidden. Then she added, 'He is a total stranger to us.'

'As is the new Earl of Comstock,' her sister reminded her.

'There is no comparison between the two. We know nothing about Mr Drake, his finances or his family. If he is single, we do not even know if he wishes to marry. But the Earl will have no choice in the matter. He must produce an heir and might welcome a helpmate already familiar with the holdings he has inherited. In turn, he will offer security,' Hope reminded her, ticking off the logical reasons she'd used to convince herself of the plan.

'So, you will sacrifice yourself to maintain the status quo.'

'It is hardly a sacrifice to marry a peer,' she said, even though it sometimes felt like it.

'It is always a burden to alter your life for the good of another,' Charity said. 'If you are doing so for my sake, it is not necessary.'

'If you don't mean to help yourself, then I must. You will not find a husband hiding in someone else's library.'

'I will be fine, with or without a husband,' Charity said. 'We might be fine together, if you will let go of the foolish idea that it is necessary to marry to be safe.'

'You do not understand…' Hope said.

'I understand more than you know. I simply do not care.'

'That is quite clear from your appearance,' Hope snapped. 'We are in London, not Berkshire. You might be required to receive visitors while I am gone. Please return to your room and do not come down again until you are wearing a new gown and a hair ribbon.'

Charity glanced in the mirror above the fireplace and then away again, unbothered by her sister's hectoring. 'The man I marry will have to love my imperfections, for I have no intention of changing my dress or my manner just to please him.'

'Then you do not know as much as you think,' Hope said. 'It is up to us to make ourselves desirable. It is not in the nature of men to compromise.'

'If a woman has enough money, they will do it quick enough,' Charity said with a nod.

'Since we are currently without funds that is not a consideration.' Not for the first time, Hope wondered if there wasn't a strain of madness running through the family. Sometimes she felt more like a keeper than a sister.

'Perhaps I shall sell some of Grandmother's jewellery,' Charity said. 'There are more than enough diamonds in her parure to spare one or two stones.'

'No!' Hope balled her hands into fists, trying to keep from tearing at her own hair. 'There will be no more pilfering from the entail. If that is the wonderful plan you keep hinting at, it is even more foolish than mine.'

'So you admit that your plan is foolish,' Charity announced, taking nothing else from the conversation.

'No!'

'Miss Strickland. Miss Charity.' Mr Drake had arrived unannounced, yet again, and was standing in the doorway, witnessing the whole embarrassing scene.

Hope pushed past her sister and grabbed him by the arm, trying to turn him towards the door. 'We need to be going. Now, Mr Drake.'

'Of course, Miss Strickland.' He pulled free of her grasp and stepped ahead of her to open doors and ready the carriage.

The bustle of the next few moments, putting on coat and bonnet, allowed her time to recover from her mortification. It was bad enough that he had caught her arguing with her sister and even worse that she'd laid hands on his person and tried to drag him from the room. If he had arrived a few minutes earlier, he'd have heard a discourse on his appearance, talents and marriageability.

Or had he heard? She had no idea how long he had been standing there, watching them fight. She stared across the carriage at him, searching his face for any trace of awareness.

As usual, his perfect face was effortlessly composed. There was no sign of clenching in that finely planed jawline. No indication that his lips, which were both firm and full, had a smile hiding in the corners. And though his eyes were alert, like a hawk scanning the distance for prey, there was no indication that the mind behind them was ruminating on a scrap of overheard conversation.

As her sister had said, he really was uncommonly handsome. It was not as if Hope hadn't noticed the fact yesterday. But now that she had a reason to study his face, it was rather like staring too long into the sun. Her cheeks felt hot and the image of him seemed to be embedded in her thoughts.

It was probably what came of staring. Ladies did not stare, even at people they wanted to look at. It was not Hope's habit to do so. Perhaps it would be better to drop her eyes and peer at him through her lashes.

But that sounded rather like flirting. She did not mean to do that, either. It was good that she was veiled, so that he did not witness her, blushing over nothing and unsure where to rest her eyes. It did no good to look lower, at the immaculate shirt front visible beneath his coat, or at his strong hands, resting casually in his lap as if waiting for the moment when they would steady her departure from the carriage.

It was growing stuffy under the veil. That was likely why she could not seem to catch her breath. Though she could not think of a rule against it, holding one's breath until it came out in sighs was probably as rude as staring. But now that her breathing had fallen from its normal rhythm, she could not seem to find it again. The first was too shallow, the next so deep that it sucked the veil into her mouth, which ended in a sputtering cough and the need to rip her bonnet away and gasp for fresh air.

Mr Drake glanced in her direction, surprised. It was clear he had not been thinking of her at all until she had called such mortifying attention to herself.

She cleared her throat and patted her chest lightly as if trying to clear her lungs. 'A bit of lint. From the veil, I think.'

He nodded in sympathy. 'You needn't wear it in the carriage, if it makes you uncomfortable. The shades are down and there will be more than enough time to put it in place when we arrive at a shop.'

'Thank you,' she said, still not sure if she wished to give up her disguise just yet.

'And, in case you have been wondering, your sister exaggerates. I did not find you overly proud on our first two meetings. Your behaviour towards me was well within the social norms.'

She had been right to worry. He had heard everything. Now, she was absolutely sure she was blushing at him. 'I apologise for the behaviour you witnessed as you arrived, Mr Drake. And for seizing your arm and forcing you from the house, as well. And for Charity's lies,' she added, for that was what they had been.

'It is I who owe you the apology,' he reminded her. 'While I did not intend to eavesdrop, that was the result of not announcing myself sooner.' He offered a shrug and another smile. 'And though I do not know from experience, I am given to understand that it is the job of younger siblings to be as aggravating as possible.'

'You have none of your own, then?' It was not her place to ask, although he had opened the subject himself, so perhaps it was not too very rude.

He shook his head. 'No brothers or sisters at all. And so that Charity does not need to quiz me tomorrow, you can assure her that I am not married, as yet, but fully intend to do so, should I find the right woman.'

'You heard everything, then.'

He nodded.

'You must think us all quite horrid,' she said. 'My grandmother was a lax guardian, at best. Since she could not be bothered to teach her, it has been left to me to be a good example to my younger sister and to instruct her in ladylike behaviour. But I have had little success.'

'Perhaps if you refrained from throwing candlesticks at her,' he said.

'It only happened the one time,' she assured him, trying not to think of all the childhood stories Charity might tell him that would sound even worse. He might never have known of them had she been able to keep her mouth shut on the previous day. 'We were rambunctious children when we arrived at the manor. At first, we did not understand the value of the items we played with. When we were old enough, Faith and I were sent away to school for a time.'

'And Charity?' he asked.

She sighed. 'She said that, if we were not going to Eton, or some other place that would prepare us for university, it was not worth leaving the house. Her manners are abominable, of course. But she is too antisocial to bother with throwing candlesticks. And she is prodigiously smart.'

'That is a comfort, I suppose,' he said.

'But it pains me that she did not go to Miss Pennyworth's Academy to learn deportment. It improved my character immeasurably.'

He smiled and touched his arm, wincing in pain. 'As I can tell from the way we took our leave of the town house.'

She readied another horrified apology. 'That was most unlike me.'

'It was nothing,' he said in a soft voice that immediately put her at her ease. 'Since you take your manners so seriously, it is unfair of me to tease you over them.'

She would have been better off to remain silent. Now, he thought her both overly proud and humourless. But either of those was better than being as nosy as her sister had been. 'On the contrary, I do not fault you for any response you might give to the conversation you heard or my behaviour towards you. What you witnessed should never have taken place. As I told Charity, it is not our business to wonder about your personal life.'

'I took it as a compliment,' he replied, still smiling. 'A total lack of interest can be rather dehumanising.'

She remembered the look he had given her in parting on the previous day, as if he had expected something more from her than an awkward goodbye. Had she been the one to treat him as less than a man? It was not as if she hadn't been curious about him. It was just that ladies were not supposed to express it openly. But if he was willing to make light of the situation, then so should she. She gave him a friendly nod, hoping that it did not look as forced and awkward as it felt. 'If it makes you feel better, I will ask you at least one impertinent question a day until we have completed out task.'

'I will look forward to it, Miss Strickland,' he said, nodding back. Then he touched his hat brim to remind her to replace her bonnet and veil. 'As I mentioned before we parted yesterday, today we will be searching for the blue painting. I have several dealers in mind, specialising in fine art. I am sure your grandmother must have visited one of them.'

The paintings in the first gallery they visited would have been more at home in a museum than gracing the walls of Comstock Manor. The owner was obviously familiar with Mr Drake, plying him with offers of tea or sherry while Hope perused artwork. She allowed herself a few moments of guilty pleasure, wishing that she had the nerve to lie and claim even the smallest of the landscapes, for any of them were likely to be prettier than the painting they were truly seeking. Then she turned back to her companion and gave a silent shake of her head.

He rose and thanked the gallery owner, then led her back to the carriage.

The next place was similar. Mr Drake was still treated with familiarity, but there were no offers of refreshment. Though the art was not quite as impressive, it was still of a higher quality than Hope had seen at home. Again, she shook her head. And, again, they moved on.

With each successive shop they moved further from Bond Street until they stopped at a shop nearly as dreary as the one that had contained the candlesticks. The ragged collection of paintings stacked along the walls no longer hid Old Masters. A few were no better than girls' school watercolours. But the shopkeeper followed close behind them, assuring them that the frames were worth ten bob at least.

Mr Drake shook his head. 'The frames are not important. We are seeking an oil painting. Something with blue in it, I think, to match the paper on the drawing-room walls.'

The proprietors of the earlier shops would have been horrified at the idea of matching art to the wall colour. But it must not have been an unusual request here, for the dealer announced that he kept the paintings sorted by colour. Then he led them to a dark and crowded corner of the shop where heavy gilt frames were stacked in precarious piles.

Mr Drake glanced at her expectantly. 'Did your grandmother say anything about the size of the painting?'

She shook her head. 'I doubt it was a miniature. But it could not have been very large, or I'd have noticed a blank spot on the wall.'

'We shall start in the middle, then.'

'Why?'

'Because they will be easier to lift,' he said, heaving a pile of paintings down from a high shelf with a grunt. They slid to the floor, raising a cloud of dust.

Hope tipped them forward, one by one, to look at the canvases. As she did so, he turned towards another shelf, pulling down more paintings, just as heavy and just as dirty.

The collected art was random, the only common denominator being colour. There were landscapes by moonlight, seascapes, a still life of berries, studies of birds, and portraits of blue-clad men and women in velvets, satins and…

She stared at the painting in front of her for only a moment, before averting her eyes in shock. Then she glanced back to be sure of its subject before calling to Mr Drake.

'I have found the painting.'

'Excellent. Let me summon the proprietor.'

She gave an embarrassed shake of her head, and pointed to the door. 'I…cannot…' She slipped her hands under the veil and put them over her eyes, sure for one mad second that if she could not see, she could not be seen by the two men in the room. Once they'd looked at the painting, they would look at her and draw the inevitable comparison.

'Are you ill?' he said, taking her arm solicitously. 'It is uncommonly stuffy here. Lord knows what ill things might be breeding on these pictures.' He tugged gently on her arm to bring it down from her face. 'You may wait in the carriage while I settle on a price with Mr Barnstable. If you are not feeling…'

He glanced down at the painting.

'Ah. Yes. I see. Please, allow me to escort you to the carriage. And I would not advise lifting your veil until you are out in the street.'

* * *

To his credit, Gregory led the girl out of the shop and into the safety of the carriage without as much as a twitch of his lips. After her prim apologies in the carriage earlier, he could imagine how she felt about the painting they had just found.

Tempting though it was to comment on them, she would not appreciate his admiration of the artist or his amusement at the subject. It would take an amazing amount of self-control on his part to sit in the carriage with her and look her directly in the eye, without bursting into ribald laughter.

Once he was back in the shop and well out of her sight, he reverted to his true expression and grinned, hurrying back to the painting for another private viewing before calling to the shopkeeper, 'Oy, Barnstable! I've found the one I want.'

The old man joined him, smirking down at the picture before jerking his thumb in the direction of the waiting carriage. 'Thought you said the missus was looking for something to hang in the drawing room.'

'We will find something anon. I am buying this one for me.'

The man nodded in approval. 'Just as well. Ain't what I'd call blue, either.'

'Mostly pink,' he agreed.

'Especially the tits,' said Barnstable.

'The scarf is blue,' Gregory said with a shrug.

'Looks more like a hanky to me. Don't cover much, do it?'

It certainly didn't. The cloth the subject was holding at her hip was barely large enough to conceal the most intimate part of her anatomy. Other than that, she wore nothing but a sly smile. Her magnificent bosom was clearly on display, as was the round of her belly, the curve of her shoulder, the hollow of her waist.

'The artist was truly gifted,' Gregory added. There was no mistaking the identity of the subject. But that was only because patches and powder had been out of style for a generation. If the woman's hair had been its natural brown, he'd have assumed it was Hope Strickland and not her grandmother. The eyes and the shape of the face were the same and the come-hither smile identical to the one he had seen Hope practising in the mirror.

If the family resemblance continued below the neck to include what was hidden under his companion's fashionable morning gown, she would not need practised smiles and rehearsed curtsies. She had but to unbutton her bodice and she could have her choice of any man in England.

'Thirty quid,' Barnstable said, still staring at the painting.

'Twenty,' Gregory countered, unable to look away.

'Twenty-five. And I'll wrap it up tight so the missus don't see what you bought.'

With the deal settled and a holland cover tied over the canvas, Gregory returned to the carriage. Miss Stickland, who had pulled the shades and removed her bonnet again, was resting against the squabs, her eyes closed.

He took his place across from her and signalled the driver with a tap of his cane and they set off for the town house.

'You have it?' she asked, not opening her eyes.

'It is tied on top of the carriage. And very well wrapped. No one need know the subject but ourselves.'

She opened her eyes suddenly and stared at him as if she'd hoped to catch him leering at her.

He had anticipated her fears and made sure

to meet her gaze with his most distantly professional expression. 'If it helps to remember the fact, I was chosen by Mr Leggett for my discretion. No one shall ever hear about what we discovered today.'

'If only my grandmother could make the same promise,' she said with a sigh.

'Things were quite different, a generation ago.'

'So I have been told,' she replied. 'At least, that is the excuse that Grandmama gives, each time something like this comes to light.'

'Have there been many such incidents?'

'None as bad as this,' she admitted. 'There is usually no one to notice but my sisters and myself.'

'I am no one,' Gregory replied.

It was a foolish thing to say. Even more so if he had done it expecting her to deny the fact and reassure him that, in the universe she inhabited, he had any kind of personal worth. Instead, his announcement was greeted with silence that remained unbroken until they reached their destination.

When they arrived at the town house, Gregory supervised the entrance of the painting himself, carrying it, still draped, past the footmen and setting it on the floor of the main salon by the fireplace. Then he waited as Hope called for her grandmother and an explanation.

The Dowager entered the room and gave the pair of them a curious look.

'We have found the painting you sold,' Hope said, frowning at her in disapproval. 'But now, what are we to do with it?'

He walked to the painting and, being careful not to look down at the canvas, pulled a corner of the holland cloth that covered it. When this did not result in a response, he pulled the rest away.

At the sight of it, the older woman clasped her hands over her bosom with a sigh of delight. 'I have not seen this in ages. Wherever did you find it?'

'Where you left it, Grandmama. At an art dealer in Seven Dials.'

'I?' She laughed. 'I would have not parted with this for the world. How often does one have such a vivid reminder of the joys of youth? I can remember the days I posed for this.' She wrapped a hand behind her neck, arching her back until her breasts pointed towards the ceiling. Then she looked back at them and dropped the pose with a chuckle. 'My arm fell asleep. It was most fatiguing. But you must admit, the results were worth the effort.'

'We did not bring this here for a reminiscence of your sordid past,' her granddaughter said with a huff. 'We have brought it home to you to complete the entail. Now where are we to put it so that no one sees?'

'The entail?' The Dowager laughed. 'My dear, this does not belong to the earldom. This was a gift from me to your grandfather. It was his pride and joy until he lost it in a card game to one of my admirers. We had quite the row over that, at the time. But that was many years ago. I have not thought of it for ages.'

'You said you sold a blue painting,' Hope said, pointing at the drape in the painting. 'We were searching for it when we found this.'

The Dowager focused in the present for only a moment. 'Oh, that. The painting I sold is nothing like this, I assure you.'

'You remember it?' Hope said, exasperated. 'Then perhaps you can give us a better description than, *blue*. Is it of a blue sea? A blue sky? A blue dress?'

'Was that what you thought I meant?' Her grandmother laughed. 'It is not a painting of something blue. It is a portrait of the Blue Earl.'

'And which one was that?' interrupted Gregory, intrigued.

The Dowager's brow furrowed. 'The third or fourth, I should think. He was sickly pale and quite ugly, with grey skin and ice-blue lips. Something in the blood, they thought. He did not live to marry. It is just as well. God knows what his children might have looked like. The title fell to a cousin and there have been no further problems.'

'You sold a portrait of a Comstock?' Hope said, amazed.

'The ugliest one,' the Dowager said, defensively. 'I do not think we have to count him. He did not last much longer than the time it took to complete his likeness. Your grandfather kept the thing behind a door in the portrait gallery because he could not stand to look at it.'

'But the new Earl will most assuredly notice when the succession of his ancestors jumps from three to five,' Hope said. 'How could you think that it would go unremarked?'

'You did not notice, did you?'

Gregory held up a hand, trying to return the conversation to the salient information. 'Was the painting labelled in any way?'

'There is a brass plaque at the bottom,' the Dowager answered.

'And his costume?'

'Jacobean. A rust-coloured leather doublet that makes his skin look truly ghastly.' She thought for a moment. 'His hair was thinning as well. Thank the Lord your grandfather came from another branch of the family tree. I loved him dearly, but I do not think I could have stood waking next to him if he'd looked like the Blue Earl.'

As he committed the details to memory, the Dowager went to the bell pull and summoned a pair of footmen, directing them to put the painting in her 'boudoir', an apt description of the sort of bedroom inhabited by a woman who would pose for such a picture. It was a credit to the loyalty of the servants in the Comstock household that they did not seem phased by any of it.

Hope Strickland watched the activity, her fists pressed against her temples as if it required physical strength to hold on to her sanity. Once the door had closed, she turned to him, angry and defensive. 'The Strickland family is one of the oldest in Britain.'

'I am aware of that,' he said, though he had no idea what difference it would make to the situation.

'We are not like *her*.' She pointed in the direction that her grandmother had gone.

'Of course not,' he said. The poor girl seemed to think it was possible to divorce herself from the woman who had given her her looks, if not her temperament. The Dowager might not have been born a Strickland, but to deny her as family was an act devoid of logic.

'If you insist on agreeing with me, you should do a better job of hiding your true feelings,' she snapped.

'I have no idea what you are talking about,' he said, giving her his most impassive smile. Then he spoiled everything by saying, 'But would it really be so bad to be like the Countess?'

'Perhaps in your family her behaviour is considered normal,' she said, her eyes narrowing.

'Perhaps it is,' he responded quietly. Since he could not name his parents, how could he know for sure? But it had been less than kind of her to point the matter out.

'Her frivolous nature is an affront to the memory of her sons, who devoted their lives to the good of others.'

'All the same, she seems most devoted to you,' he said, amazed that she could so easily dismiss the love that he'd longed for during his own, lonely childhood.

'If she truly cared for us, she would behave as the rest of the family did,' Miss Strickland replied, unimpressed. 'My father was a vicar who gave his life helping others. As did my mother.'

'It must have been very difficult for you,' he said, wondering if that was why she was so enamoured of self-sacrifice.

'Had he lived, my eldest uncle would have been a peer, committed to the well-being of his tenants and loyal to the Crown.'

'I am aware of that,' he said, wishing that she would let him forget the differences between them, even for a moment. It would serve her right if he pointed out that her uncle's demise made it impossible to know whether he had been a paragon or subject to the human frailties of an ordinary man.

'And the last of the three was at Talavera,' she finished. 'He died a hero.'

'Of course he did,' Gregory said, unable to contain his sarcasm any longer.

'What do you mean by that?' If he'd meant to insult her, he'd succeeded, for she sounded even angrier with him than she had been with the Dowager.

'I mean that it is a perfectly logical choice for a second son to go into the army when he is given the money for a commission.'

'But you could not afford one,' she finished, mocking him just as he had mocked her family.

'On the contrary. I had more than enough money to be an officer,' he snapped. 'But I do not like following orders.'

'Then it is most curious that you have put yourself at the beck and call of every gentleman in London,' she retorted.

She made him sound like a lackey, which was probably just how she thought of him. 'Let me clarify. I do not want to follow orders that will get me shot as a traitor, should I refuse them. More so, I do not want to follow orders that will get me killed when I obey. I am sure your uncle would be more humble than you are at his heroism, had he survived it. But he did not.'

'The men of my family were not afraid to give their lives in service to others,' she said in a soft, warning tone.

So she thought him a coward? Then let her. 'I do not wish to be a martyr for any cause, no matter how noble. My goal is to live to a ripe old age without leaving unacknowledged sons or impoverished daughters who must throw themselves on the first title that shows interest.'

'I doubt you will have to fear leaving a full house,' she bit back. 'You would have to marry before you get a widow and I cannot imagine a woman who would have you.'

'You cannot imagine?' He reached out and took her arm, forgetting his plan to keep his temper and his place. 'Perhaps it is because you are so sheltered you confuse prudishness for virtue.'

'There is nothing wrong with me,' she whispered. Perhaps it was true. Though when she shuddered at his touch it was with desire and not fear.

'There is nothing wrong with me, either,' he murmured in response. 'When I am ready to marry, it shall be to a woman who wants a man instead of a title. A woman who could appreciate this.' Then he closed the last of the distance between them and pulled her into a kiss.

Even as it was happening, what was left of his normally rational mind announced that it was a terrible idea. He had been goaded into an argument that had nothing to do with him and everything to do with her fear of seeing a body so like her own displayed as an object of desire.

But that was what she was.

It did not matter that she was an innocent, or that she was so far above him in birth as to make a romance between them laughable. She was everything that had enticed his father, nine months before he was born. Had he known where it was, Gregory would have sworn on the grave of his mother never to make the same mistake. But now that the moment had come to resist temptation, he did not just choose the path to ruin, he raced down it without hesitation.

Perhaps there was a weakness in his blood, just like the Earl in the missing painting. The taste of Hope Strickland's mouth was like the boiled sweets he'd stolen as a child. She was all the more delicious because she was forbidden. The body that was crushed to his would be pillow soft and silk smooth under her gown, the most delightful resting place for a man both inside and out.

He felt her gasp against his lips as her mouth opened and he took advantage of it, slipping his tongue between them, filling her mouth. Her lashes fluttered against his cheek like the wings of a moth and her soft moan of alarm changed almost immediately to one of pleasure.

If he'd thought to prove some point, to assert some sort of dominance over her, he'd succeeded. It was time to let her go. His conscience laughed at the very idea. He had not done this to win an argument. He'd done it because it was what he'd wanted, from the first moment he'd seen her. Nor did he wish to stop, now that it had begun. He would not be finished with her until her body had revealed its last secret to him. With such a woman, the exploration might take a lifetime.

A lifetime?

This was madness. In a week, he would be working for someone else and she would go back to practising smiles for a cousin who might never arrive. He pulled away, trying to free himself before he was trapped for ever. But it was already too late. He was panting as if he'd run a mile. His body stirred as if they were tethered by some invisible bond and he could use it to draw her back into his arms, where she belonged.

They stood for a long, silent moment, a pace apart, staring at each other. He waited for an angry response, a stinging slap, a shriek of outrage. Or perhaps a scream of violation.

Instead, she stared at him with wide, confused eyes, her lips still parted as if the kiss had not ended. Perhaps she was still too shocked to put him in his place. Or perhaps she wanted more.

It did not matter what she wanted. The kiss had been a risky mistake that would grow even more dangerous if it was repeated. For all he knew, his father still bragged about the memory of seducing a beautiful woman. But his mother had not understood that she would lose her life as well as her reputation. If Hope Strickland could not call a halt to what was happening between them, it was up to him. Once again, he must do his job and rescue a member of a noble family from themselves.

This time the service would not just be gratis, it would come at great personal expense to his pride.

He allowed himself a last moment of melancholy pleasure. Then he looked at her and wiped his mouth with his hand as if to rid himself of the taste of her lips. 'But no matter what my future might hold, I will not be wasting any more time on you than is absolutely necessary.'

'I…don't understand,' she whispered, touching her lips with her fingers.

'What is there to understand? You are a tiresome little girl who must brag about her dead relatives because she cannot tolerate the perfectly human mistakes made by the living ones. I would not spend five minutes in your company if I was not paid to do so. And I certainly will not be kissing you again.'

'Did Mr Leggett pay you to kiss me?' she said, her brows furrowing in confusion.

'Do not be ridiculous.'

'Then you did that on your own?'

'And I will not do it again,' he repeated, waiting for the rejection to register on her face.

'Then you had best go,' she said, still staring at him as her fingertip traced the curve of her lower lip.

He stared back, watching the slow movement of it along the edge of that soft, wet mouth. Then he forced his eyes away and pushed past her, towards the door and freedom.

Chapter Five

It had been one of the most embarrassing and confusing days of her life. It was one thing to hire a discreet agent to help with the family's financial difficulties and quite another thing to let him see the matriarch unadorned and unashamed, even if it was in oil and not flesh.

The painting never should have existed. But since it did, her grandmother could have spared her some embarrassment by being ashamed, or at the very least modest. And he never would have seen it if they had not been looking for another painting which should have been hanging in its proper place in the family gallery, back in Berkshire.

The whole incident had been mortifying. But if she was honest, Hope had to admit that it had been made even more so by her own

behaviour. If she had been as composed as
Faith or as oblivious as Charity, Grandmama's painting might not have bothered her.
She would not have become agitated or shrill.
She would not have started spouting off about
family honour to the point where she seemed
vain and condescending.

But then Gregory Drake would not have
kissed her.

And what was she to make of that kiss and
the things he'd said afterwards? He'd implied
that there was something wrong with it. Or
perhaps that there was something wrong with
her.

Perhaps there was. She had no right to be
complaining about something her grandmother
had done to please her husband, only to follow
it by kissing a man who had not even asked
to dance with her, much less wed her. And
she had opened her mouth while she'd done it,
which did not seem like the sort of kiss a nice
girl would give, even after marriage.

Even worse, she had enjoyed it. All of her
anger and frustration had disappeared at the
first touch of his lips, replaced by something
warm and delicious. If she had any criticisms
at all, it was that it had ended too soon.

Then, he had announced that he wanted nothing more to do with her. He had stormed out of the house without saying goodbye. But in the middle of the afternoon, a large flat package had arrived containing the painting of the Blue Earl who was every bit as hideous as Grandmama had said. There was a letter attached, addressed to her.

Dear Miss Strickland,
With the Dowager Countess's more complete description, I was able to locate the appropriate painting with ease. I had but to return to the shop we already visited and request the ugliest portrait available.

I was led immediately to the Fourth Earl of Comstock.

Despite herself, she had smiled. Then she'd continued reading.

After the events of this afternoon, I think it is best that I continue the search for the missing items on the list without your help.

My behaviour towards you in the salon of your home was inexcusable.

When I was hired by your family, there was an expectation that I would treat you with respect. In both my words and actions I have failed abominably.

Please be assured that, should I decide to resign from the assignment, I will not be telling Mr Leggett the whole truth of my reason for doing so. I will say that it is too difficult, or too inconvenient for me to finish. Both might be true. But the matter of this afternoon is between us and us alone.

Should I decide to continue, I will solicit the Dowager's help with the remaining items. It is possible that she will be more truthful to a person outside the family than she has been to you.

The truth of that had stung almost worse than Mr Drake's earlier rejection. Was she really as bad as he had claimed this afternoon, so judgemental that her own grandmother did not want to speak to her?

She'd returned to the letter.

As I left today, I said that I would not waste my time on you. I regret these words more than any others I spoke for

*they imply that you were in some way
at fault for what happened between us.*

*Any guilt or blame for today must rest
completely on my shoulders. I am sorry
that I proved to be the unworthy companion that you suspected I was and I give
my word that I will not inflict my presence on you in the future.*
Sincerely,
Gregory Drake

Now, as she dressed to go out for the evening, she was just beginning to accept the
truth.

He had abandoned her.

She had suspected that it was happening as
he had stormed out of the salon. She had convinced herself that perhaps things were not as
bad as they seemed. As usual, she had been
wrong. He was gone and the thought of it left
her utterly bereft.

Their efforts to complete the entail would
not be enough to solve her problems. But until
the Earl arrived from America, it felt good to
be doing something. It felt especially good
to be doing that something with Mr Drake,
who made the search feel more like a trea-

sure hunt and less like a hard slog towards inevitable failure.

And then he had kissed her.

He had carefully avoided any mention of the kiss in the letter, which was currently tucked beneath the lining of the jewel case sitting on the vanity table in front of her. Even if someone bothered to search for it, they would not really know what had happened. But that meant neither would she. He did not explain why he had kissed her. He did not tell her if he'd felt anything other than embarrassment afterwards. And he had hinted that her feelings about it should be something between outrage, insult and disappointment.

As her maid, Polly, wrapped the stays around her body, Hope glanced in the direction of the hidden note, wishing it had been a *billet doux* instead of an apology. She would likely be married without ever receiving one, while Grandmama probably had boxes of them. She sighed.

Then, at the prodding of the maid behind her, she took a few deep breaths to prevent being laced into an uncomfortably tight corset. Some girls did not even need one. But Hope had the same sort of physique that had been so flagrantly displayed in the picture that Mr Drake should never have seen. As with so many gifts from her grandmother, she could never decide if it was a blessing or a curse. She took another deep, overheated breath and the maid loosened the lacings again before knotting them and dropping petticoat and ball gown over her head.

Hope took her seat at the dressing table and Polly began to undo the curling papers and arrange her hair. When she looked up at her reflection in the mirror, she saw Charity standing in the doorway, leaning against the frame.

'You should be dressing,' Hope said, attempting a disapproving nod that was cut short by Polly's tugs on her curls and the caution to be still. 'Lord Ellingham's ball is this evening and we will be leaving as soon as we have finished with my hair.'

'Correction,' Charity said. 'You and Grandmother will be going. I will be staying here. I am right in the middle of a most interesting passage in one of the Comstock journals I found here and I cannot be interrupted.'

'We did not bring you to London so you could tuck yourself away in a different library,' Hope said, approving the finished coiffure and dismissing her maid. 'You are supposed to be looking for a husband. You cannot do that if you do not leave the house.'

'As I have said before,' Charity answered, 'no one will want me without money. It is better that we spend this Season focused on your prospects.' Then she smiled, as if changing the subject, though her tone remained exactly the same. 'Did you have an interesting day with Mr Drake?'

Hope could not contain her blush. 'Did Grandmama show you the painting?'

'She showed me both of them,' Charity said. 'But I assume you are asking about the one she sat for. Or laid for, rather.' She threw one hand behind her head and rested the other between her legs.

'You should not have looked,' Hope said, shaking her head.

Charity shrugged. 'Everyone else did. Even Mr Drake.'

Hope winced at the memory and felt her cheeks grow hot.

Of course Charity noticed. 'And what did he think of the picture?'

'He was too polite to give his opinion,' Hope said.

'Is he always so gentlemanly?' Charity was staring at her as if she had already guessed the answer to the question. When she had that look in her eye, there was little point in trying to evade it. The interrogation would be relentless until she learned what she wanted.

Hope surrendered. 'He kissed me.'

There was no pause of surprise before the next question. 'Where?'

'On the lips,' she said, annoyed at the satisfied sigh that accompanied the words.

Charity responded with a huff of irritation. 'Where were you standing when it happened?'

'In the salon. Grandmama had just taken the painting upstairs and we were alone.'

Her sister leaned forward, her smug superiority momentarily forgotten in perfectly girlish curiosity. 'Did you like it?'

Hope bit her lip. 'Proper young ladies do not ask such questions, nor do they answer them.'

'I will take that as a yes,' Charity said with a satisfied nod.

'I should not have,' Hope said quickly. 'It happened so fast that I did not know how to stop it. But it ended quickly as well.' Which still felt strangely disappointing. 'It should never have happened at all,' she said firmly. 'And when it did, it was wrong to take pleasure in it.'

'Do not be ridiculous. Kissing is usually considered pleasant, or people would not bother to do it. You can hardly control a visceral response,' Charity said and slowly closed her eyes. 'And he does seem to be the sort of man who could evoke feelings.'

'Yes,' Hope admitted. Perhaps it was his fault, after all, for being too handsome to resist. 'But I am still not sure why it happened. He did not seem very happy afterward.'

'Considering his past, I expect he was not,' Charity said, acting just as she always did, as if she knew more than everyone in the room.

Hope sighed. 'Go ahead. Tell me what it was about his past that would make him unhappy to have kissed me.'

'I will if you tell me what it was that set him off.'

Was there any part of the day that had not been mortifying? And must Charity tease out every last secret? 'I was overwrought,' Hope said at last, shaking her head. 'After seeing the painting and Grandmama's reaction to it. It was humiliating. She could not contain her pride, even in front of Mr Drake. What must he think of us?'

'So you went on a sanctimonious rant about our honourable family heritage,' Charity retorted, making a face.

'Between her pilfering and her lewd paintings, Grandmama does not do a very good job of protecting our family reputation.'

'And you felt the need to explain it all to a natural son whose family would not claim him and who is now being paid to clean the Strickland linen,' she said, then stared at Hope, waiting for her to understand.

Hope had not thought it was possible to be more embarrassed by what had happened, but apparently, she was wrong. 'I had no idea he would think my words pertained to him. He must have thought me the most arrogant woman in the world.'

'It is worse than that,' Charity added, her smile even wider.

'Of course it is,' Hope said in a faint voice. It was as if, because she had enjoyed a kiss, God meant to punish her by spoiling every other moment in the day.

'Of the parents, his mother was the proud lady and his father the underling who seduced and abandoned her. I suspect he was appalled to find he was acting out a tradition from his own family, right there in the salon.'

'He will never want to see me again.' That was what the letter had said and what he had meant by it being all his fault.

'If he is attracted to you, what he wants to do might be quite different from what he actually does,' Charity announced.

'He is not attracted,' Hope corrected. 'He said that he would not have spent a moment with me had he not been paid to do so.'

'That is quite possibly true,' Charity said. 'If he had not been hired by Mr Leggett, there is a good chance you would never have met. But now that you have, the fact that he is employed by the family makes no difference. It does not make him less than human. And it certainly does not make him any less of a human male.'

He was definitely that. Hope could not help the little tremble of excitement she felt when she thought of the strong hands that had grabbed her and pulled her into his arms.

When the cloud of fantasy cleared, she

looked up to see Charity was staring at her as if she was an idiot. 'He kissed you because you are a beautiful woman and he *wanted* to kiss you,' she said, explaining it as if it should be obvious. 'His passions were likely inflamed by the presence of the picture which bears a striking resemblance to you. There were also the ideas I might have put in his head...'

'You told him to kiss me?' said Hope, horrified.

'I told him not to,' Charity said with a dismissive wave. 'Rather, I told him not to seduce you. Telling a person not to do a thing is often the same as urging him on.'

'Why would you do such a horrible thing?'

Charity grinned. 'Because when as fine a masculine specimen as Gregory Drake enters the house, someone ought to get a kiss from him.'

'And you decided it should be me?'

'You are the most insufferably proper girl in London,' Charity said. 'And I hope your tiny fall from grace will make you stop treating Grandmother and me like a pair of unrepentant sinners.'

'You must not tell Grandmama,' Hope said hurriedly.

'Of course not,' Charity agreed. 'Though I suspect she will applaud the incident, just as I do. But now that it has happened, we must decide for ourselves what you are to do about this.'

'We?' Hope said, shocked at her sister's audacity. 'You have done far too much already. From now on, any decisions will be mine alone.'

'And Mr Drake's,' Charity added.

'He has made his decision already,' Hope said, trying not to sound sorry for herself. 'He wrote to me to apologise and says our outings have proved too dangerous to my reputation and he will have nothing to do with me from now on.'

'I see,' said Charity.

But that sounded suspiciously like she had been rejected. It would be better if the parting was a sensible, mutual decision. 'And I do not plan on doing anything with him, either,' she added.

'Of course not,' Charity said with a definitive nod and a smile that belied it.

'I may not ever see him again,' Hope added.

'And it is probably for the best. I cannot kiss him again, even if he should want to. It would not be right.'

'Because you are going to marry the heir,' Charity said with a resigned sigh.

'That is still the most logical thing to do,' Hope said. 'Then it will not matter as much if Mr Drake leaves us, or if the entail is incomplete. I will explain everything once we are married and ask for forgiveness.'

'Must you always try to think three moves ahead?' Charity asked. 'You are not particularly good at chess.'

'My skills are more than adequate. They might actually appear so if I was not always playing against you,' Hope explained as patiently as she was able. 'And while you are quite good at outsmarting me, I am still the elder. I need to think of others as I plan my actions. I cannot just fall in love, willy-nilly, with the first man that walks through the door.'

'Unless he has a title,' Charity finished for her, turning towards the door. 'Enjoy the ball, Sister dear. And try not to make too many conquests while you are there. It would be cruel to Mr Drake.'

'He does not matter.' Hope rushed to the door and leaned out into the hall, shouting at her sister's retreating back. 'And I do not matter to him.'

Chapter Six

Despite Charity's advice that she enjoy herself, Hope did not expect the evening's party to be much better than tedious. As the weeks of the Season crawled by without the arrival of her cousin, she'd come to view the events she attended with a kind of distant dread. She had to be on guard at all times, not wanting to have too much fun or enjoy herself so completely that she forgot her *raison d'être*. She must not lose her heart or her head, or cause a similar reaction from any of the gentlemen present.

If it seemed to be happening with Mr Drake, it was simply a sign that she had not been cautious enough. This was a reminder to be ever vigilant.

It was exactly the opposite of the advice she

received from her grandmother, who sat opposite her in the family coach. 'Above all things, make merry, my dear. You are only young once. Now that Mr Leggett is providing for us, it is finally possible for me to give you the Season you deserve.' Her grandmother was wearing the faintly worried look she got sometimes when the matter of money came up.

'There was nothing wrong with the opportunities you provided for me in Berkshire,' Hope said to reassure her. 'The house party at Christmas was delightful.'

'That was for Faith's engagement,' the Dowager replied. 'If Mr Leggett had not invited himself to it, there would have been not one eligible man in attendance. And if not for him, Faith might have married that dreary Mr Fosberry.'

'He was not so bad,' Hope lied. Then added, 'But I am glad she married Mr Leggett instead.'

'Without a proper come out, with new gowns and a ball, Cyril was the only offer she got, and she had to trap him into it,' her grandmother added. 'Perhaps, when she and Mr Leggett return from Italy, we might persuade him to throw a ball for you.'

'I am quite content to wait until we can celebrate the arrival of our American cousin,' Hope claimed, smiling to hide any bitterness she felt. A year ago, she had wanted nothing more than a party swarming with eligible bachelors. Then there was no money for it. Now, there was no need. Either the Earl would marry her, or they would all have to settle for spinsterhood and rustication.

'Do not wait for anyone,' her grandmother insisted, patting her hand. 'Dance every dance. Find a balcony or a terrace, or at least the shade of a potted palm, and be alone with someone, just as all the other couples do. And if you break some young fellow's heart, be sure it is not before giving him a reason to remember you fondly.'

'You are not supposed to suggest such things,' Hope reminded her. 'You are to tell me to guard my virtue like a precious jewel.'

Her grandmother made a puffing noise in response and then grinned. 'Jewels are of no value if they are never put to their intended use.'

'Your metaphor is weak. Jewels are just as valuable if they remain in the lockbox,' Hope remarked. 'At least when they are there, one can be sure that they have not been lost.' She had resisted the temptation to substitute the word *sold*. If Grandmama had understood that, they would not be in the trouble they were in now.

The Dowager finally seemed to sense her thoughts. When she turned to look again, the older woman's expression was still loving, but faintly wounded. 'I know you do not approve of me, my darling. Perhaps I am a trifle too rackety to raise young ladies. But I was quite good at raising sons. They are easier, you see.' As they drove moonlight and shadow flickered over her face and her expression seemed to change the happy and rather foolish woman Hope expected into someone else who was much older, wiser and sadder.

Hope turned her hand to close it over her grandmother's. 'You have done well with us, Grandmama. It is I who am not as grateful as I should be. I promise, I shall dance every dance and have as much fun as I am able, without breaking any hearts at all.'

One broken heart a day was more than enough.

Hope had been looking forward to the Ellinghams' ball for reasons that both Charity and their grandmother would have considered sorely misguided. If it went in the manner of all the other balls she had attended this Season it was likcly to be an entire evening where nothing of interest happened at all. Tonight, that suited her well.

She stood in the doorway to the ballroom revelling in the utter predictability that awaited her. There was no need to make polite introductions for there was no one here she had not seen a dozen times before. She could perform even the most complicated of dances without missing a step. Even the conversations would not vary from those she had had several times this year. She would not have to think about the entail, the Earl or Mr Drake for four long hours.

It would be heaven.

In the past week, she'd had far too much to think about and too many strange new feelings. With each new day, her life seemed to get more complicated, not less. Perhaps, now that she had driven Mr Drake away, things could go back to the way she had planned. Why could she not find comfort in the thought?

'Hello, Ellingham. Lovely evening.'

'Hello, Drake. As always, it is a pleasure.'

Hope clutched the door frame, afraid to

turn towards the men talking in the entry-way just behind her. There was no need. One was her host. Though the other had been a stranger a week ago, she knew the sound of his voice as well as she knew her own.

Why was he here? Had he followed her? It seemed unlikely since he'd wanted nothing to do with her just a few hours ago. Perhaps he had more than one employer. If so, she had no right to enquire as to his presence here. It was possible that he would not even want to acknowledge her should they meet.

She definitely did not want to see him. At least, not until she could manage to compose herself. She could feel the colour rising in her cheeks already. It would not matter whether they spoke or not. The whole room had but to look at her face to know that there was some-thing between them.

Run!

She was not sure where she meant to go, but she could not stay where she was. In a moment, he could step forward and be at her side. She looked frantically around, spied a corridor to her left, darted down it, grabbed the first door handle she saw and slipped into the unlocked room, shutting the door behind her again with a soft click.

The music and chatter of the ballroom faded to a distant murmur. She was safe, isolated from the crowd and the one man she could not bear to see. But where was she hiding?

She turned slowly to examine the room. Apparently, she had chosen Lord Ellingham's study as her bolt hole. It was unoccupied and likely to remain so, for the only light came from the embers of the banked fire.

If she stayed here for just a few minutes, Mr Drake would disappear into the crowd. While she waited, she could prepare a proper response in case they met. She could practise it in the mirror, just as she did for the Earl.

The thought made her smile. It was a shame she did not have Mr Drake's composure. Other than those few moments in the salon, he had been unflappable. He had threatened to quit the job, but she doubted he would. There were still three items left on the list the Dowager had given her. She could not imagine that he would give up before he thought the job had been completed, no matter how awkward the interaction between them had been.

Or perhaps there were only two items.

She stared at the desk in front of her and the inkwell sitting on top of it. She had seen it hundreds of times in the same spot on her grandfather's desk in his study at the manor.

Hope's palms itched with the urge to grab it and run. Why should she not? It belonged in her family home, not in the house of some bargain hunter who graced his desk with castoffs from the Lombard merchants. Even better, she would be able to show Mr Drake that she was not totally reliant on his help. The quicker she could reclaim the items on the list, the sooner they could be truly free of each other.

As it had this afternoon, the idea of his departure raised a strange mix of feelings in her, both anticipation and dread. It was another sign that he should go. She had never been so confused by the presence of a man in her life. Who knew one kiss could cause such disruption?

If she hoped to leave the room at all this evening, she must not think of the kiss. There were more important things, right in front of her. She moved closer to the desk to get a better look at her prize. It was exactly as she remembered it: a graceful well of rock crystal, set upon a gold filigree base.

She held her reticule against the side, pleased to see that it was just big enough. She uttered a brief prayer for forgiveness for the theft and swept the thing off the desk and into her purse. She hurried back to the door, opened it slowly and glanced both ways up and down the hall to make sure she would not be seen escaping. Then she stepped out of the room and walked briskly back towards the ballroom.

'Miss Strickland.'

She froze in her tracks. 'Mr Drake?' How had she not noticed him in her brief search of the corridor? She turned slowly to the sound of his voice, with a smile that she was sure was nowhere near as convincing as the one she had while practising in her own home.

He was standing in an alcove, outside in the hall, and just out of sight of the study door. No. He was not standing. He was lounging, his posture as casual as that of any other young buck at this party. His dress rivalled theirs as well: immaculate blue coat, buff breeches, snowy linen and a cravat that was not just white, but *blanc d'innocence virgi-*

nale. It crossed at the front, not even tied, the creases and folds at his throat in perfect and crisp alignment as if he held them there by dint of his own considerable will.

'I did not expect to see you here this evening,' she said. Her voice was embarrassingly breathless.

'I assumed as much, from the way you ran into a private room to avoid me.' So this was no chance meeting. He had been waiting in the hall to catch her doing something she should not.

Or perhaps he had been waiting for his chance to do exactly what she had just done. He had come to retrieve the inkwell. Her smile relaxed as she imagined his surprise to find her one step ahead of him. She opened her fan and gave it a coy flutter. 'My dear Mr Drake, you are mistaken. I was not avoiding you. I was doing what you have obviously come to do for yourself. Now that it has been taken care of, there is no reason for you to remain.'

He gave a surprised laugh. 'You are dismissing me?'

Thank God, he understood. And she should thank God as well that their relationship had returned to being dull and professional instead of dangerously exciting. 'Yes,' she said, pointing towards the front door with her fan. 'You may go.'

He raised a hand to his face, cupping his chin and drawing a single finger across his lips as if to seal in the laughter that seemed to be happening somewhere deep inside him, for his shoulders shook and his eyes sparkled like sunlight dancing on choppy water. When he had regained control of himself sufficiently to speak, the hand fell away. 'Or, I could stay.'

'I do not think that will be wise,' she whispered. 'What if someone sees us speaking?'

'I do not know,' he whispered back. 'Perhaps they will think you are flirting with me.' Then he raised his voice to a normal tone. 'It will be much less intimate if we do not whisper. Even less so if we return to the ballroom, where the rest of the guests are gathered.'

'The rest of the guests?' Perhaps he misspoke, for that almost seemed to imply that he belonged there.

'I am sorry,' he said with mock surprise. 'I assumed you were invited as well. I must compliment Ellingham for the novelty of hiring a young lady to guard his door. Was I expected to bring the card he sent? I left it at home for my valet said it quite spoiled the line of my suit.'

'You have a valet?' It had been an exceptionally stupid question, but it was too late to call it back.

'Since my skills do not extend to pressing coats and starching linen, I thought it sensible to hire one.' His eyes hardened, ever so slightly and his smile chilled. 'I also have a butler, a housekeeper, a cook and as many footmen and maids as they deem necessary to effectively run my house.'

'Oh,' she said, softly. She had not given any thought at all to Mr Drake's living arrangements. Nor had it occurred to her that he had friends who might welcome his company. She had certainly not expected to find that they had any in common. She was as bad as Charity claimed if she assumed he appeared like a djinni, then disappeared again, existing only to serve her.

Before she could frame the apology that he so richly deserved, he was speaking again. 'But you must forgive me, Miss Strickland. Since we have met tonight, I have talked of nothing but myself. How are you, Miss Strickland? And how did you come to be sneaking out of Lord Ellingham's study? Most importantly, why is your reticule leaking ink?'

'Oh, dear Lord.' In her rush to reclaim the family property, she had ignored the purpose of the item she took. 'I forgot to empty it.'

He was staring at her. It was clear the explanation was not sufficient. 'It's the inkwell. The Comstock inkwell,' she added, for clarity. 'Grandmama sold it. Lord Ellingham must have found it in the shop and bought it. I was retrieving it from the study.'

'With Lord Ellingham's permission, of course.'

That would have been the sensible thing to do. She could have written him a letter tomorrow, requesting the chance to purchase it back. Instead, she had decided, on a moment, to take it now. 'No,' she admitted.

'You stole Lord Ellingham's inkwell.' He was staring at her now as if he could not quite believe the words he'd just spoken.

'I did,' she said, horrified.

He held out his hand, resigned. 'Give me your reticule.'

He had been here to enjoy an evening with friends and she had embroiled him in a burglary. 'You should not have to...'

'Give it to me,' he said firmly.

She held it out and he took it from her, pinching the strings between two fingers of one white gloved hand. 'Now go to the retiring room and get yourself cleaned up. You have ink on your hands.'

'Oh, dear.' Her own gloves were likely ruined, just as the reticule was.

'We will speak later,' he said.

Actually, she rather hoped they would not.

Chapter Seven

When Gregory had been offered triple his fee to deal with Hope Strickland, he should have taken the warning and run, as far and as fast as his legs could manage. After finding the blighted painting of the Blue Earl and shipping it to the Comstock town house along with his apology, he had sat down to write a letter to Leggett in Italy, tendering his resignation.

One of his favourite things about the job he had made for himself was the lack of awkward attachments once the task was finished. He had been left with casual friendships, of course. But there was no scorekeeping, guilt, recrimination, or even embarrassed gratitude attached to the things he had done for them. Once the bill had been paid for a service, all behaved as if it had never happened.

But when one started kissing the employer's family, one should quit the employment. Even if it had been an accident. Even if it was not going to happen again. Even if…a hundred other excuses and conditions he had run through trying to explain what had happened this morning.

Even if he never saw Hope Strickland again, there was no way to forget what had happened this afternoon. Perhaps it was a sign of an inherited weakness of character. Perhaps it was only her extreme desirability. But the more aloof she became, the more he wanted to ruffle her feathers. The more untouchable she appeared, the more he'd wanted to tug on the one wayward curl that she could not seem to stop worrying at.

And the more covered she was? The more he wondered if the body underneath matched that of her worthy ancestress. Tonight's gown was nothing like the modest day dresses she wore to go about with him. The primrose net clung to her full hips and the décolletage was so deep that a man could lose his soul it.

And her reticule was covered with ink. What had she been thinking?

She had been trying to escape him, of

course. And trying to prove that she could do the job he'd been hired for as effectively as he could, so she might never have to see him again. When talking to him had been unavoidable, she'd assumed that he must be working. Why else would Gregory Drake be associating with decent people in the evening?

The answer to that was that he knew many of them and counted most as friends. He was invited to so many balls and routs that it was surprising he had not already made an acquaintance with the Strickland sisters. It was also sensible, now that they were in the same place, that he made sure she had been introduced to all his eligible friends. That was well within the parameters for the other half of his job: setting her cap and mind for anyone who was not the Earl of Comstock.

It was also the last thing on earth he wanted to do. When he had seen her disappear into a darkened room, his first, unworthy impulse had been to follow her and lock the door behind them. It had taken several minutes of internal struggling to focus on the only thing that should come to mind when he saw her: his job.

Now that he had regained control of himself, he returned the inkwell to its proper place, taking the time to clean up the spilled ink. Then he wrapped the spoiled reticule in a handkerchief and handed it to a footman, giving instructions that it be returned to the Strickland carriage to await its owner.

Once finished, he proceeded to the ballroom where he'd meant to be all along. He helped himself to a glass of punch, which Ellingham House always served strong. He had a second glass for good measure. Then he joined the dance to do the thing he had promised himself he would never do again. He needed to talk with Hope Strickland.

It did not take him long to manoeuvre himself into a position where the only natural thing to do was to offer to partner her. She looked around frantically for a moment, hoping to find someone who she might claim to have promised a dance to. Then she gave up and accepted defeat, and his arm.

They danced in silence for a moment before he said, 'You do not have to be frightened of me, you know. There will be no embarrassing repetition of this morning's incident.'

Did she look disappointed? If so, the expression passed almost instantly. She stared at his hand. 'How do you keep your gloves so clean?'

'I beg your pardon?'

'I ruined mine. The maid in the ladies' retiring room could do nothing with them and found me a pair to borrow for the evening. But you...' His hand touched hers as they cast down the set and she stared at it in amazement.

'I was very careful,' he said, when they met again. At least, he always had been, before he'd met her. 'Your reticule is in your coach and your brother-in-law will be billed for my ruined handkerchief. Also, Ellingham's staff will be missing two table napkins tomorrow.' He shrugged. 'A lesser inconvenience than a missing inkwell, I think.'

'You returned it?' She frowned.

'Because it did not belong to you. That particular style was a popular gift to servants of the Crown in the middle of the last century. The engraving on the base indicated that it was given to Ellingham's grandfather.'

He hoped it was only embarrassment that caused the dramatic scarlet flush in her face. For a moment, he feared she was becoming ill. 'I am mortified,' she murmured. 'And sorry to you as well. I should never have proceeded without consulting you.'

That was perfectly true. But it pained him to see her suffer over the mistake. 'You were precipitous in your actions, but they were somewhat helpful. Now that I have seen an example of the thing I am seeking, I shall have no trouble finding it in the shops I frequent. It shall be delivered to your house tomorrow, by noon.'

'You are too kind, Mr Drake.' Perhaps it was because she'd been veiled for so much of their time together that he found it so affecting to look into her eyes. They were the warm brown of a good sherry and just as intoxicating.

He felt himself flushing under her gaze and hoped it could be blamed on the warmth of the ballroom. 'It is nothing, Miss Strickland. I am simply doing the job I have been hired to do.'

'And I seem to go out of my way to make it more difficult for you,' she said. 'This afternoon, when I spoke of my family, or bragged, rather…'

'You have a right to be proud of them,' he said. He should not have had the second glass of punch. He was straining to smile, revealing too much of the man behind the façade he'd created to deal with his employers.

'Charity told me of your past. I did not mean to draw an unfavourable comparison between your life and mine, and I am sorry if it seemed so.' She reached up with a free hand and brushed at the stray curl, which was no more out of place than the rest of the soft ringlets surrounding her face.

He stared at it for a moment, watching in fascination as it caressed her cheek and then bounced away again. 'If I took offence, I am the foolish one. And as for what happened next...'

'You promised that we would not speak of it,' she reminded him, though she seemed more surprised than scolding. Had the reminder of their kiss pleased her? The smile that danced across her lips was more playful than practised.

He smiled back. This time it felt as relaxed and natural as moving through the patterns of the dance with her. 'I merely wish to reiterate my apology.'

'It is accepted,' she said. 'But you must stop taking all the blame on yourself. I was horrid to you.' She touched the curl again—clearly it was a nervous habit. 'And this evening, I treated you as if you did not belong here. I would not have been surprised if you refused to speak to me ever again. And yet you still helped me.'

'I would not have bothered you, had you not needed my help,' he reminded her.

The dance had ended, but their conversation had not. Out of the corner of his eye he could see several fellows moving forward to take his place. Before they could arrive, he held out his hand to her again.

Without a thought, she took it and they lined up for the next set.

'It is good that you did help me,' she added. 'Tonight, I thought to show you that I could manage alone. But I did not do very well, did I? I did not even notice that the thing I took had someone else's name written upon it.'

'I have been dealing with such problems far longer than you have,' he reminded her. 'Checking for details is almost second nature, as is keeping my head clear and my gloves clean.' He stopped himself before he could say more. What had begun as reassuring a client was beginning to sound suspiciously like bragging about his abilities.

'What seems natural to you is just short of miraculous to others,' she said. Her gaze dropped to the floor for a moment. When her eyes met his again, he felt the same euphoric jolt as he'd got from Ellingham's punch.

'Of course, Grandmama's list is nothing compared to other problems I am facing. I will need an actual miracle to solve them,' she said.

He waited through another series of steps, but she made no effort to enlighten him.

'If there is something bothering you that Mr Leggett was not aware of, I am sure he would want you to tell me,' he offered.

When next they passed in the dance, she was biting her lip, as if trying to decide. Then, she shook her head. 'The only one who will be able to help with this matter is the new Earl of Comstock. It is why I am so eager to meet him.'

'Of course you are.' Because all the things he had done for her, and all he might do in the future, had no value when compared with a title.

The dance ended, and he escorted her to the edge of the floor. Once there, she gave him what she probably thought was a sympathetic smile. 'I mean no disparagement of your abilities. But this is a family matter.'

As if all the things he had done so far were not. 'Just how well do you know your esteemed cousin, Miss Strickland?'

'Better than you do, I should think.' She was bluffing, of course. She knew nothing at all.

Until Gregory received responses to the enquiries he'd made, he knew little beyond the fellow's name. So he bluffed as well. 'I wonder, do you want to know the truth about the man you are saving yourself for?'

'I am sure there is nothing that will surprise me,' she said. But now her smile was the one that looked strained.

'I do not think you do,' he answered, strangely satisfied to have riled her.

'If you know anything, speak,' she challenged. 'But I think it is far more likely that you are just trying to be difficult.'

'Do you doubt my word?' She had every right to, since he had nothing beyond vague hints to offer her, yet he could not help continuing. 'Your brother-in-law hired me because of my abilities. I can find things that no one else can. Candlesticks, for example. And paintings. And inconvenient truths.'

'Then reveal them,' she snapped as all her earlier goodwill evaporated. 'It is your job to do so.'

'What would your response be if you learned that the future Earl was full seven and seventy?' A hypothetical question was not precisely a lie.

He watched her trying to suppress a shudder before replying, 'We cannot all be young and handsome. It is unfair to judge a person with only a single detail to describe them.'

It only became a lie when he embroidered over the half-truth. 'Then I will add the gout that has delayed his crossing, the excesses that brought it on, the bad temper resulting from the continual pain and what has been described as a difficult nature by his friends and employees.'

The beautiful girl beside him swallowed and there was a long pause as she tried to choose a response that did not reveal her obvious disappointment. 'People exaggerate for any number of reasons. You cannot know any of this firsthand, therefore you have no way of proving them.'

Now was the point where a man of honour would admit that he had spoken falsehoods in anger. Instead, he blundered on, jealous at her defence of a man she had never met. 'I suppose you will still doubt when you meet his wife, who must be old enough to be your mother since she has presented him with four daughters and a son. All but the oldest are unmarried and will no doubt enjoy a London Season along with the opportunities that his title will bring. What they will not appreciate is competition on the marriage mart by a pair of distant cousins.'

'Married.' He had expected her to look disappointed. Perhaps there would be a few bitter tears that her plans would come to naught, the kind of small tantrum as one often saw from pampered creatures used to getting their own way. Then, she would turn her sharp tongue on him, blaming the messenger as she had done after they found her grandmother's portrait.

He would deserve it for the foul way he'd just treated her. Had he learned nothing from this afternoon? Had the truce they'd forged on the dance floor meant nothing at all?

But tonight's response was far worse than

the stunned silence that had greeted him after their kiss. Nor was it the slight upset he had expected tonight. No minor shock could have caused the sudden pallor of her face, or the stricken look in her eyes. For a moment, he feared she might swoon right there in front of him. It did not seem as if she was going to cry. Rather, she seemed to be doing a brave job of holding it back, as if she knew that once the first tear escaped, there would be a flood that could not be staunched for several hours.

'I am sorry,' he said, ready to call back every word of the last few minutes if it could erase the pain he'd already caused her.

'No,' she said, firmly, placing a hand on his arm as if she were the one to offer comfort. 'I will be all right. It is far better to know the truth than to nurture false hopes.'

But had they been false? There was still a chance that things were just as she believed and a stranger was coming to rescue her from across the sea. Or it could be just as he predicted. How could he recant, if he did not know the truth himself?

She swallowed again, and he saw the supreme effort it was costing to maintain her smile, which was every bit as lovely and as false as the one she'd practised in the mirror. 'The family is fortunate that he has been blessed with a son. The succession is secure and we needn't worry about the future.'

'But you and your sister...' he began to say.

'It was kind of you to think we might be competition for our new cousins,' she said, patting him on the hand. 'But I doubt they will have anything to worry about on that front. As long as he is kind to Grandmama and allows her the dower house, Charity and I shall find a way to manage.'

'Do not worry.' There was only one thing to do that could make this right. Now that it had occurred to him, it seemed to be the most sensible thing in the world. It would justify his rash and uncontrollable behaviour, whenever he was around her. If this was where he had been heading, since the first moment he'd seen her, his life made sense again.

The middle of someone else's party was no place to make an offer of marriage. But he must say something to assure her that one was coming. He grasped the hand that covered his. 'You and your sister will want for nothing.'

'Of course not,' she said, as if she had not heard. Then she gave him another dazed and dazzling smile. 'And now, if you will excuse me... I am not well.' Then, before he could say the words he needed to, her hand slipped from his and she walked away.

Hope sat in the darkened coach for hours, listening to the chuffing of the horses and the occasional jingle of their harnesses until, at last, the ball ended and she was driven to the front of the house to retrieve the Dowager. As she usually was after an evening in society, Grandmama was tired but happy. Her face was rosy and her every breath seemed to exhale in a sigh of contentment. 'I swear, that was the most delightful evening I've had in ages. The food was excellent and the musicians played not a single note out of tune.'

'I am glad you enjoyed it,' Hope said, unable to keep the bitterness from her voice. 'It may be the last one we have.'

'Do not be melodramatic, dear.' The old woman smiled at her and shook her head. 'You young people. Every problem is the end of the world to you.'

'It is the end,' Hope said, trying to make her understand. 'Mr Drake knows something of the heir coming from America. He is married.'

'Good for him,' came the cheerful reply.

'It means he will not want me, Grand-mama,' Hope said urgently. 'His auditors will find the missing items and I will not be able to stop what happens next.'

'With Mr Drake's help, you shall have them all back in time, I'm sure.'

'But not the diamonds, Grandmama.' Could it be she had actually forgotten them? 'He does not even know they are missing, much less where to look for them. What has become of the Comstock parure?'

The Dowager gave her a puzzled look. 'It is in the lock room at the manor. You know I do not like to wear it. It is too heavy.'

'You do not wear it so no one will notice that the stones are paste.'

Her grandmother glanced out the window at the passing scenery, acting as if she had not heard. 'The moon is exceptionally bright to-night. It is a shame we are not in the country for it would be a beautiful drive.'

'You must tell me what you did with the diamonds,' Hope urged. 'If I know where to look, maybe there is some way we can get them back before he arrives. But if I can-not influence the heir... If he doesn't want to make me his Countess... There is no way we can guarantee that the secret will be kept. What if he is angry? What if he wants the money for them?' She reached out and took her grandmother's hand, squeezing it in encouragement.

After what seemed like an eternity, the Dowager turned her head from the window to acknowledge that she had heard the questions put to her. 'Hope, darling, do not worry. It will all turn out for the best. These things usually do, you know. But I have nothing to tell you on the matter of the diamonds. Please do not ask me again.'

Chapter Eight

Mr Drake returned the next day, promptly at ten.

It was a relief to see him because Hope had awoken feeling something rather like optimism. Given the reality of circumstances, the feeling was totally misplaced. But she could not help the contents of her dreams, which had been illogically happy.

The same man who was now walking up to her front door had figured prominently in them. They had been dancing together at the ball. And as he had last night, he had told her the horrible news about the Earl. But then, just as her future seemed darkest, he had smiled at her and taken her hand, pulling her out of the set to the gasps of those around her.

'Do not be afraid. You shall want for nothing. I have a big house with servants and room for your sister.'

He had actually said most of those things last night. But he had not taken her in his arms and kissed her, as he did in the dream.

It had been a wonderful dream. But she was awake now. No matter how handsome he was, with the sun shining on the fringe of his gold hair, he was not going to stick one of his immaculate gloves into his pocket and produce the Comstock diamonds. They were doomed. All three of them.

At least, she suspected so. She knew what happened to thieves. But what happened to their granddaughters? And was the punishment any less for dowager countesses? It might simply be disgrace and public ostracism. That would be bad enough, but it was better than Newgate.

Mr Drake had reached the door and she opened it as he reached for the knocker, startling him. 'You were watching at the window,' he said with a surprised smile that she could not manage to return.

'Soonest started, soonest done,' she said, hurrying out to the carriage where a groom was pulling down the step for her.

'I am glad you are feeling better,' he said, his smile flattening to an upward quirk at the corners of his mouth, and offered a hand to help her up into her seat.

'I beg your pardon?'

'Last night. When you left me, you said you were ill.'

'Oh,' she said softly. She'd had no idea what excuses she had made for leaving. After he had finished destroying her hope for the future, the evening had devolved into a miserable blur.

'We both knew you were not sick,' he reminded her. 'I upset you with my talk of the heir.'

'It is all right,' she said quickly, feeling her stomach lurch as the carriage began to roll.

'No, it is not,' he said. 'Last night...' he started to say, then paused to wet his lips.

His hesitance was unusual for he was rarely at a loss for words. She raised her veil so they might talk face to face, since whatever he wished to say must be important.

'Last night, the things I said to you were not true.'

'You received conflicting information?' she

said, surprised to feel more uneasy than relieved by the reversal of fortune.

'I lied,' he said with a resigned sigh. 'It was cruel of me to taunt you and I never would have done so had I known how it would upset you.'

'You lied,' she repeated. 'But why?'

Again, he paused. Again, he wet his lips before speaking. 'It bothered me that you seemed to prefer the help of the Earl to anything I might offer.'

'You were jealous.' Now she was not just surprised. She was amazed.

'Yes,' he said. Then he added, 'Professionally speaking, of course.'

'Of course,' she repeated.

'I do not know any more about Miles Strickland than I did on the first day. He might be exactly as you hope him to be, single and eager to help you.'

The prospect should have made her feel much better about the future. Instead she felt a vague disappointment. 'He might also be exactly as you described him,' she replied.

'But we will not know for sure until he arrives.' He reached a hand out and covered hers in a gesture of reassurance.

She stared down at it. It was a nice hand. She had never been conscious of male anatomy before, especially not the extremities. When she thought of them at all, she imagined her father's hands, which she could remember as pale and gentle, or her grandfather's, which were thin and knotted. When she attended balls, the hands of the men she danced with seemed to have no weight to them at all, barely grazing hers as they danced.

But Mr Drake's gloved hand was solid and strong. It did not tremble as it lifted her into carriages. It had been faintly possessive as it had led her through the dance at the ball and it had not hesitated when forced to take her reticule and return her stolen goods.

She had seen the bare skin briefly, when he had removed his gloves to root through the chest of candlesticks with her on the first day. They had been darkened by sun with a smattering of freckles across the knuckles. The nails had been clean and neatly trimmed, but there was something about them that made her suspect he was not afraid to get dirt under them, if a task required it.

All in all, she'd have described his hands as 'capable'. Much like the rest of him, really. He met problems without flinching and dealt with them. It was what he'd been hired to do. He was not helping her by choice. He was doing it for money. No matter what she had dreamed, she must not expect anything more than that from him.

He cleared his throat and she started suddenly, aware that she had been staring at him.

He pretended that he had not noticed and removed his hand to pull the list from his pocket. 'I thought today we might try to find the oddment.' He gave her an expectant look.

She nodded in agreement, eager to turn her mind to a problem that might have a solution.

He offered an expectant wiggle of his fingers, staring at her in a much more forthright way. 'I thought, perhaps, a description would be forthcoming by now.'

'It would if I had one to offer,' she replied. 'Grandmama is mum on the subject, but assures me I will know it when I see it.'

'Oddment implies that it is a remnant of something,' he mused. 'Or did she use the term in a more general manner? Could she have meant an oddity?'

'I really have no idea,' she said. 'And if I

cannot tell you what it is, then I cannot even
tell you where to begin to look.'

'Then, I will take the initiative.'

Despite herself, those words made her feel
instantly better.

He thought for a moment. 'There are several shops I can recommend that sell things
no one else has. Let us assume that, whatever
this thing is, there is not another like it in the
whole of London.' He looked at her sideways
for a moment. 'You may find these places
rather unpleasant. They are not the sort that
one normally takes gently bred young ladies.'

'I find the whole experience rather unpleasant,' she said with a sigh. 'Why should this
day be any different?'

He held up his hands in surrender. 'You
have made that clear. Just know that I am not
doing this in an effort to upset you, again. You
have been warned.'

Would it disappoint him, she wondered, if
the more horrible he made it sound the more
tantalising it became? Sometimes it seemed
that the most interesting experiences were
things that gently bred ladies were not supposed to do. Like kissing, for instance. No
matter what Charity thought she knew on such

subjects, it could not have been as satisfying as practical experience.

The shops they visited today were a different sort of revelation. Who knew there was a store in London that had an entire cupboard full of stuffed owls and the largest spider she had ever seen, preserved under a bell jar? Or that there was another place specialising in music boxes and clocks that had complicated animations on the hourly chimes? At that place, there were some cases he flatly refused to allow her to look into, insisting that though the mechanisms were clever, they would shock her worse than her grandmother's painting had.

But since the Comstock heirlooms tended neither to taxidermy nor automatons, they could not help her. None of the many fascinating things she saw were the Dowager's oddment.

But at the third shop, she felt a familiar rush of excitement. There were Roman coins and lapis scarabs, and fragments of Greek statues. There were so many fingers and ears and arms and legs that she wondered if it might be possible to put them together like a life-sized puzzle.

And suddenly, she knew what they were looking for. 'Excuse me.' She stepped forward to interrupt the conversation of the shopkeeper and Mr Drake. 'Excuse me, sir. But do you have any more Egyptian artefacts?'

'In the box.' He pointed towards the marble.

'Those are mostly Greek. The thing I am looking for will be in a wooden box. Ebony, I think. With a gold ankh inlaid on the cover.'

At his blank response, she traced the symbol in the dust on the counter. 'And it is held shut by leather bindings.'

The man grinned at her. 'I did not take you for a connoisseur, miss.' He reached behind the counter and brought out a thing she had never expected to see again.

She smiled and held her breath as she opened it, fearing that the contents might have disintegrated with age.

Mr Drake leaned over her shoulder to look as she raised the lid and recoiled in disgust. 'What the devil is it? And why would anyone want the thing back?'

'My great-grandfather did not stop at the Grand Tour. He went all the way to Cairo!' she said with pride.

'And dismembered a mummy?' The look of

revulsion on the handsome face at her shoulder was properly impressive.

'Do not be such a ninny.' She waved it in his face and watched him jump. 'It is not a real toe. It is a false one. Made of ebony with a gold nail.' She ran a finger along the bindings. 'It fit around the foot just so and strapped on with these.'

'There are still bones,' he said. 'I can hear them rattling.' His face was bloodless white and he was still backing up.

'I do not know how you could. You are almost out into the street. And those are not bones rattling, they are the metal tips of the laces. Now come back here and pay the man.'

'Put it away, you ghoul.' He shuddered. 'Or you will never see me again.'

For the first time in what felt like ages, she laughed as she had when she was a child. Why had she ever stopped? Was there some rule that young ladies did not succumb to mirth? Or had she created one just for herself? No matter. She must remember to break it more often. She rolled her eyes at Mr Drake and put the prosthetic back in the box, closing the lid. 'There. All better?'

'Somewhat,' he agreed, reaching for his

purse. 'We are taking that directly back to the town house, for Leggett is not paying me enough to ride around London with that abomination in the carriage with me.'

Once they'd returned home, she took the box to the library and left it beside the sofa that was Charity's habitual place. 'She will be so amused to see it again,' she assured him with an evil grin. 'I used to chase her around the house with it, when we were small. She retaliated by hiding it under my pillow one night. I did not sleep for a week.'

He stared at her, disgusted. 'What sort of women are you?'

'Ones that were moved suddenly as small girls to a house with few playthings,' she said, patting the box with affection. 'Until we settled in and Grandmama bought us proper toys, we had a most exciting time rummaging through the family heirlooms.'

'Are there any others as ghastly as this?' he asked.

'None that you will be forced to retrieve. The last item on the list is a porcelain vase and it is really quite ordinary.'

'That is a great relief,' he said, with a half-smile.

'And now I understand Grandmother's cryptic description of it. She could not abide the thing. We agreed to have a funeral for it, if we could have a proper Egyptian one with a burning barge.'

'Egyptians have pyramids,' he supplied. 'You are confusing them with Vikings.'

'I know. But we wanted a fire,' she said. 'It was most disappointing. In the end, we settled for a hole in the ground and a tapered stack of stones on top.'

'You were allowed to bury it?' he said, surprised.

'Grandmama encouraged it. She said it came from a grave and, as decent Christians, we should put it back in one. We recorded it in the family Bible so that future, less squeamish Comstocks could find it.'

'And then she dug it up,' he stated.

Hope shook her head in amazement. 'She hated the thing. She must have been quite desperate for money, if she chose to retrieve this.'

'Though it was not first on the list, I'll wager that this was the first thing she took,' he mused.

'How can you tell?'

'Because it was as good as gone already. No one would miss a thing that had been given a formal burial. Who was likely to go looking for it?'

'When the Earl's agents came to do the audit, I would have told them the family story and shown them the Bible,' she said, surprised.

'And they would likely have left well enough alone,' he concluded. Then he added, 'But I am glad she decided to include it in the list. It makes things so much easier when the people who hire me do not hold back important details.'

'Oh,' she said. He was probably referring to their conversation from the previous evening. She wished he would stop hinting about the matter since she doubted there was anything that could be done without the help of Comstock. She gave him the most innocent look she could muster. 'Are people often less than forthcoming?'

'By the time it is necessary to bring in an outsider to sort out the mess, you would think that there would be no energy left to cover things up.' He shook his head. 'But there is always some small hope that the situation, whatever it is, will resolve itself without my help.'

'Or they know that it cannot be fixed,' she replied. No matter how much money Mr Leggett had given him, he could not have enough to buy back the huge stones in the Comstock necklace.

'Or they are ashamed,' he added.

It certainly explained her grandmother's behaviour.

'They needn't be,' he said softly when she did not reply. 'They have no reason to be so. If the mistake was someone else's, then any guilt rests with that person and not the one trying to help.'

'Thank you.' Even this tiny bit of absolution was a comfort. How had Faith managed for so long, when she had been the only one to know of the family's troubles? The money her marriage had brought made things easier. Yet, after less than a month of trying to rescue the Dowager, Hope felt near to exhaustion.

'I think it is because they do not fully trust me,' he said. 'I am not *of them*. Had it been my father who was of noble birth and not my mother, I might have been an acknowledged member of a noble family. I would never have had an earldom, but at least I'd have been able to tell you my true name.' His steely-grey eyes softened with sadness.

Was that what he thought the problem was? That she did not think a bastard was worthy of her secret? 'That is not the problem at all,' she insisted. 'I think you are the most fascinating man I have ever met and I trust you with my life.'

'Then prove it to me,' he urged.

Before she could even think to speak, she had kissed him.

Chapter Nine

They were like an ember, dropped on to dry leaves. For the shortest of moments they were still two separate things and it might have been possible to stop what was happening. And then they were one and they were on fire.

His hands came up to cup her face and he returned her kisses, on the mouth, on the cheeks, and eyes and hair. Then he bit her earlobe and groaned. 'I will never let you regret this. I swear on my life.'

How could he even think that she might? It was too wonderful to be sorry over. She wrapped her arms around him, laid her head on one of his strong, wide shoulders and all the worries of her life seemed to melt away.

His hands came away from her face and she felt them behind her and the little jolts of movement as he stripped off his gloves and threw them to the floor. Then his bare fingers were stroking the back of her neck and twining gently in her curls. 'Some night, soon, I shall come to you and pull all the pins out of your glorious hair. Then, I shall make you tease every inch of my body with it.' His lips returned to hers again and his tongue slipped into her mouth.

It was as it had been the last time. Only it was even better. Charity was right. He had lied when he said he wanted nothing to do with her. If his words had not convinced her, the power of this kiss would have left no doubts. She tried to mimic his movements, to thrust her tongue back against his, and heard the gratified moan of response.

Then he was pulling her backwards and they half-sat, half-fell on to the library sofa in a tangle of arms and legs and bodies. She was on top of him, almost in his lap. Her skirts must have risen well past her knees for she could feel the fabric of his breeches moving against the bare skin above her garter.

She should at least pause to arrange her dress. But if she had cared at all about modesty, she should not have kissed him in the first place. Nor should she be squeezing a man's leg between her thighs as she was now. It felt good to have him there, to have any part of him pressing upward to a spot that was more sensitive than it had ever been before.

His hands were on the fastenings to her gown, undoing them, pushing it down her shoulders so he could mouth the naked skin of her throat and lick his way down to the top of her corset. He ran a finger along the upper edge and inside it. His kisses slowed and he murmured, 'When I am sure we can be alone, I will have you out of this. Then, I will take all the time I like with these. I will suckle you until you beg me.'

She wanted that. But what would she be begging for?

Her body seemed to know. She was suddenly aware of her own hips, rocking against his breeches, riding his extended leg in a way that sent a strange trembling through her body.

He did not push her away. Instead, he responded by clasping her bottom with both hands, urging her to continue and sucking her lip between his teeth.

The sensation of that bite travelled directly to the place she was so eagerly stimulating and she moaned in surprise. The feeling was wicked and wonderful, and she should put a stop to it immediately. But for some reason, it was quite impossible. It was as if she was no longer in control of her body.

She heard him chuckle against her mouth and he pulled away from her, staring into her eyes with a devilish grin. Then there was a rustling as he pushed her skirts up even higher, letting his hands roam freely over the bare skin of her hips and thighs.

She froze, shocked. 'What…' It was all she could manage to say. The rest of her thoughts were drowned in a gasp as he bent his knee and held her hips still so he could stroke her between the legs with the top of his thigh. She did not know what was happening to her. But by the look in his eyes, it was clear that he did. Now, he was urging her to move, pinching her to make her squirm against him. And suddenly, her breasts, still constrained by the corset, felt as if they were held in the firm grip of a man's hands.

Gregory Drake's hands. Skilful. Clever. Hers.

He held her as she bucked and rubbed against him like some wild animal in a frenzy.

Then, the tension in her broke and an uncontrollable shudder raced through her, a spasm of newly discovered muscles, followed by a rush of ecstasy that went on and on, long after she'd stopped moving.

When she had recovered sufficiently to be aware of anything other than the tingling place between her legs, she noticed the hard, insistent bulge in the breeches she was resting against.

She looked up, frightened.

His smile was strained, but satisfied. 'I think we have had enough fun for the day. If you will excuse me, for a moment?' Carefully, he disentangled himself from her skirts and left the room.

She could not decide whether to be relieved or disappointed by his words. Had her behaviour given him a disgust of her? What had she been thinking to act that way at all? She took advantage of his absence to try to rearrange her clothing and compose herself. But her gown still hung loose about her shoulders for she could not reach the tiny buttons to close it again.

When he returned, his posture had changed to be almost serenely relaxed. It was only when he looked at her that she noticed the true difference. There was a possessiveness in his gaze, and a trace of smug satisfaction to his smile. 'Let me help you with your gown.' He came to sit behind her and did up the fastenings as quickly as any lady's maid.

Then he laid his hands on her shoulders. 'How are you feeling, Miss Strickland?'

She felt magnificent. She wanted to answer back with the same cream-fed cat's smile that he gave to her, pretending to him and to the world that she had some control over the emotions still rioting through her. Though his hands were now touching her quite innocently, she felt as the Dowager had looked in the painting, naked, shameless and wanting more of whatever it was that had just happened. 'How do I feel?' she said at last. 'I am not sure, Mr Drake.'

He turned her gently until they were sitting side by side on the sofa. It was really quite proper, except for the absence of a chaperon and the fact that he had been making love to her just moments ago.

She turned to him, suddenly worried. 'Was that what is meant by losing one's maidenhead?'

She must have said something foolish for he laughed, just once, before gaining control of himself and giving her a patient smile. 'There is much more to it than that, my dear Hopc.'

She could not decide what she liked better, being called by her Christian name or being called dear.

'Technically, you are still innocent,' he added. 'You would not be asking that question if you were not.'

'Technically,' she repeated. She did not feel innocent. She felt like Jezebel and Bathsheba, all rolled into one.

'While what has been learned cannot be unlearned, we did not actually...' He paused, probably sensing her eagerness for more forbidden knowledge, and thought the better of giving it to her. 'There is no physical evidence of what we have done. Only the knowledge that certain touches will bring you great pleasure.'

'So, we might do that as often as we liked?' she said and knew immediately by the shocked expression on his face, that it has been exactly the wrong thing to say.

'That would not be wise,' he said, sucking on his lip as if the words tasted bitter. 'It becomes quite difficult to stop these things, once they are started.'

'But if we did stop,' she said, 'no other man could tell what we had done together.' Could that even be possible? She was sure that, if she looked in the mirror, the change would be plain on her face.

'No other man?' he said, surprised.

'Well… Yes. If I were to marry, would my husband still think I was a virgin?' she said, putting it plainly so he might understand.

'Yes, Miss Strickland, you are still a virgin.' He stood up suddenly, running his hands down the front of his clothes in one sharp swipe, as if it were possible to shake the last hour out of their lives along with the wrinkles in his coat.

'Mr Drake.' She held out a hand to him, hoping he would come back to her.

Instead, he walked to the place where he'd dropped his gloves, scooping them up in one brutal move. 'As always, Miss Strickland, your manners are impeccable. One must never call a gentleman by his first name, even after he has put his hand up one's skirt.'

'Gregory,' she corrected.

But it was too late for that. He was pulling

on his gloves with short, sharp, angry tugs. 'There is only one item left on the list for me to find. I am confident that I can retrieve it without bothering you for your help, if you can provide a more detailed description. I will leave my direction with your butler so you might send me the information by post. Good day, Miss Strickland, and goodbye.'

Once outside, Gregory waved off the hired carriage so that he might walk home. Or rather stalk. He wanted to stamp the whole way back to Wimpole Street where he could stamp to the brandy bottle in the study and slam every door on the way.

Damn Hope Strickland. Damn all women, for that matter. Never in his life had he taken such risks with his own livelihood. It was not bad enough that he had flirted with a woman from a family that employed him, he had compromised the honour of an innocent.

Even worse, he'd done it in broad daylight in a public room where they might have been interrupted at any time. Her younger sister haunted that library like its resident ghost. It had been a miracle that they had been alone together there long enough for anything to happen. Had Charity appeared, he would have educated both sisters on things that neither should learn before marriage.

It would have been even more embarrassing to be found taking a hand to himself in a nearby retiring room. But considering the state he'd been in when she finished, a release had been necessary, if only to prevent him from bringing the interlude to a more mutually satisfying conclusion.

Of late, he'd spent far too much time polishing his sword after visits with Miss Strickland, trying to maintain the control that had been shattered today. He had not planned for what had happened. He had hoped to encourage her to be honest and reveal whatever it was that had troubled her so on the previous evening. He had wanted to be her confidant, nothing more than that. He had asked for her trust.

Instead of the truth, she had given him a kiss. More than a kiss. She would have given him whatever he wanted. She had been more than eager to follow wherever he led. And what a sweet creature she had been. She had thoroughly enjoyed what they had done and made it clear from her questions that she had never experienced such a thing before.

He should have thrown her down on the hearth rug and shown her what it meant to be ruined for other men. Then, when he'd made the offer that had been on the tip of his tongue since last night, she would not have ruined it all by asking how best to appear innocent for the next fellow.

How big a fool was he that he'd thought there was some deeper meaning in what they'd just done? He was not just willing to marry her, for the sake of honour. Damn him, he wanted to do it.

It had always been his plan to marry, but he had thought of it as a distant thing, a crowning accomplishment to his success. But what more was needed to satisfy him, or his future wife? He had a house and no one to share it with and more money than he could spend on his own.

If he had been waiting to fall in love? He was not sure he believed in that particular emotion. But he would not be so foolish as to deny the existence of desire, which he felt each time he saw Hope Strickland. That was more than enough to be going on with.

If passion died, there would still be the protectiveness he felt each time she gave a worried tug on her hair. It made him want to take her away and show her just how pleasant it might be to take care of a husband and children, compared to a lunatic family that merely acted like children.

After he'd pleasured her today, he had come strolling back into the room, cocksure of his chances when he made his offer. But by the time he had managed to do up her gown, she'd been thinking of the Earl again. Truth and gallantry was rewarded with a kick in the teeth.

Eventually, Comstock's heir would appear. Then, if the man was young and single, or even old and single, she would do what she had planned to do all along and throw herself at him.

At some point, he had forgotten that his primary job was to complete the entail. He had become so wrapped up in the idea of the troubled and beautiful Hope Strickland that he had been willing to break every rule he'd ever made for himself. He had violated the trust her family had put in him, lying and seducing, taking advantage of a woman never meant for him. He was becoming the man he had sworn he would never be.

Tomorrow he would grab the first vase he could find that might suit the Dowager's list. Then he would leave Miss Strickland to sort out her own future, just as her sister had suggested he do. He would write to Leggett immediately and inform him of his resignation. Never mind what such an abrupt end might mean to his reputation. It could be no worse than what might happen if he lost control again and took Hope to bed.

Once he was free and did not have to see her every day, he would recover his equilibrium. Momentary madness had made him irrational, and willing to abandon his dearest principles in quest of a woman he could never have.

His thoughts of marriage were nothing more than an attempt to salve a guilty conscience. If he had been in his right mind, he would have seen that his offer would have been met with a surprised *no*.

The whole escapade had been a result of man's basest emotions—pride, envy and lust—as if he could not resist committing deadly sins in the presence of a woman named for a virtue. It was not, nor could it ever be, more than a huge mistake. For how foolish would he have to be to fall in love with Hope Strickland?

Chapter Ten

Gregory Drake was gone again and Hope was still not sure what she had said to drive him away. In fact, she had understood very little about the last hour of her life, other than that it had made her happy and that, for a few moments at least, she had been convinced that her problems no longer existed. Everything was going to be all right because Gregory Drake would make it so.

He had called her Hope and she was sure she had not responded properly to that. By the scowl on his face as she had called him Mr Drake, he had wanted to hear his name on her lips. She should have realised it. But was that the sort of error that could make a man leave for ever?

He must have thought her terribly stupid

for asking the questions that she had, but she had needed some clarity. What they had done seemed like the sort of thing that should result in a proposal and she could not exactly compound one transgression with another by demanding that he marry her.

Apparently, it had not been necessary for him to offer. She was sure that what had happened between them was improper. But it was also an easily kept secret. There was no physical evidence and he was not the sort of man who would tell anyone about it.

She, on the other hand, desperately needed a confidant. There was much she still didn't understand about what happened between men and women. A girl from a normal family would have been able to ask her mother, but she'd lost hers a decade before such questions had occurred to her. Barring that, she should ask Grandmama.

And what a disaster that would be. The last thing Hope needed was a story about what had happened on that same sofa, a generation ago. If she refused to keep her own life secret, how could Hope trust that she would not brag to the world that her granddaughter was following in her notorious footsteps?

Faith would explain things properly. Faith was married and married women knew things. Sometimes they whispered secrets to each other, just as unmarried girls did. But it was easy to tell by their knowing looks and sly smiles that what they said was to be shared only amongst the matrimonial sorority.

Faith could help. But Faith was in Italy and could do nothing for weeks. Hope needed someone now.

That left Charity. It vexed her that she should have to go to the youngest member of the family for advice. But though the Lord had failed to bless her little sister with beauty, he'd more than made up for the lack with intelligence. She'd learned more from books than any of them did from experience. She would know what had happened and what to do about it. She could tell Hope what must be said to bring back Mr Drake, beyond calling him Gregory in the letter he was expecting.

But where was Charity, if not in the library? It was past lunch and she was always here by now. But she had not been here when they arrived, nor had she greeted them from any of the rooms they'd passed on returning home. A quick check of the house proved she was not writing letters in the morning room, nor in the kitchen pestering the cook for an early tea.

It was most curious. Perhaps she was ill and had decided to remain in bed for the day. Hope walked up the stairs and knocked softly on her sister's door, calling her name. When there was no response, she knocked more loudly. When there was still no answer, she tested the handle and opened the unlocked door to find the room empty. A letter lay on the perfectly made bed, its edges aligned with the pillow in mathematical precision. Her name was printed across the top in Charity's hand, perfectly legible and devoid of any feminine affectations or flourishes.

Before she unfolded it, Hope had a horrifying premonition of what she would find inside.

Dear Sister,
While I would not go as far as to call our stay in London delightful, it has at least been interesting. While the townhouse library is small, it has given me a chance to explore several unexpected lines of enquiry that I will explain to you should they be productive.

*But no further action can be taken
here. Thus, I have decided to retire to
the country until further notice. Thank
Mr Leggett again for the money spent in
trying to launch me. His heart is in the
right place, as is yours. As I keep trying
to explain to you, my time and my future
should be my own. It is better spent in
our own library in Berkshire.*

*Do not concern yourself with my safe
travels, as the journey is not a long one.
I am taking the mail coach and I will
likely be home before you find this letter.
My regards to Grandmother and Mr
Drake,*
Charity

As usual when dealing with her youngest sister, Hope was torn between the desires to scream in panic or scream in frustration. Charity had many deficiencies of character, but the greatest was her overconfidence in her own abilities. She rarely bothered with protecting her reputation, declaring that no one would notice or care if she ruined herself. In choosing public conveyance over the Comstock carriage with a maid and livery, she was thumbing her nose at propriety and tweaking her sister's nose as well.

Something had to be done. It was unlikely that Charity needed rescuing. She was correct in that it was a short trip. But if her luck had run out and she had embarrassed herself or the family, the damage would need to be repaired.

Even if she was lucky, she needed to be persuaded back to London as soon as possible. Someone had to explain to her that the manor was no longer her home. She could not simply retreat there whenever she had a mind to. While they had not spoken of it, the family plan had been to seek other lodgings once the Season was over.

Mr Drake had apologised for lying about their future, but there was a chance that he had guessed it correctly. There might be several young Stricklands on a ship right now who would be bringing maids or valets, clothing and furnishings, planning to occupy the bedrooms she and her sisters had been using. Even if the new Earl did not bar the door against their return, she and Charity might be expected to make way for the heir's own family. Someone needed to tell her little sister the news in a calm and reasonable tone that she would understand and accept.

Hope did not feel up to the task. She did not want to lead her wayward sister back into the fold. She wanted to strangle her. Grandmama would be useless in any attempt to rein in Charity's recklessness. She had declared years ago that there was no point in lecturing the girl since she was unlikely to listen and clever enough to evade any punishment that man could devise.

What was to be done? Hope tapped the folded letter against her leg in agitation, wishing she had any other answer than the first one that came to mind. Then, she went to the writing desk and composed a letter to Mr Drake that had nothing to do with missing vases.

'I do not know what you expect me to do about this,' Gregory said, staring down at the letter from her sister that Hope Strickland had handed him. It was easier to do that than to look at her. As always, she was beautiful. But today, there was a vulnerability in her huge dark eyes that made him long to kiss it away.

'Bring her back,' Hope replied.

He stared at her, waiting for her to elaborate. When she did not, he asked the reasonable question, 'Why did you not go to the Dowager with this problem? It is her responsibility to chaperon your sister, not mine.'

'She is not here, either,' Hope said, her mouth set in a frown of disapproval. 'When I went to search her out, the servants said she had gone out of the city to visit a sick cousin and would not be back for a day at least.' She threw her hands up in exasperation. 'She simply disappeared without saying a word to me on the subject.'

'And what would you have done, had she told you?' he asked, trying not to smile.

'I'd have told her to stay right where she was, of course. Or she might have taken Charity with her. If my sister refuses to find a husband, she should be encouraged to do good works and to develop some sort of natural, feminine feeling towards the rest of the family.'

'Like a proper spinster, you mean.'

'It would not hurt my sister to read to an invalid, on occasion, instead of thinking only of herself.'

'I see.' He cleared his throat in what he hoped was a sombre manner. But he could feel his lips twitching in amusement at the sight of the left-hand curl bouncing furiously in time to her agitation.

'But they do not give a fig for my opinions. They go off in opposite directions like hens in the garden and they leave me to decide what to do about it.'

He suspected they did not think she should be doing anything at all, other than waiting for their return. But clearly, Miss Hope Strickland felt that action was required. If Faith Strickland had been anything like her sister, he felt a deepening understanding of James Leggett.

'Your letter said to come at once. That you needed me urgently,' he reminded her. 'You offered me no clue as to what this was about.' And he had made an ass of himself. He had come running, foolish enough to think that she might be longing to repeat what they had done on the library sofa. As usual, it seemed his urgent need for her was quite different than what she felt when she thought of him.

'I do need you, urgently,' she said. And finally, she realised how she had sounded, for she stopped speaking and turned crimson with embarrassment. Her brown eyes seemed to grow even larger than usual, pleading as she stared back at him. 'I know you are angry with me from before. And whatever I did to offend you, I am sorry for it. Really, I am. But Mr Leggett hired you to help our family and I do not know how to handle this on my own.'

So she had no idea what she had done to him, any more than she understood that she must phrase professional enquiries differently from love letters. And now, she had no right to look so soft, so vulnerable and so helpless that he wanted to scoop her into his arms and make love to her on the spot. Especially if she meant to stand up afterwards and look for another, better man.

He cleared his throat again and tried to put the idea behind him. 'Leggett's instructions to me were quite plain. There was nothing in them about policing Miss Charity's behaviour.'

'You were hired to retrieve things that are missing. She is missing.'

'She is not an item,' he responded. 'And you know exactly where she is.' He was tempted to assure her that the odds were slim that the girl had been set upon by white slavers on the mail coach to Berkshire. But then he would likely have to explain what that meant to her.

It would not make the situation any better to put ideas into her head.

'Now you are just being difficult.' She frowned and balled her firsts on her hips to show her displeasure with him. But the gesture only served to accent her curves and remind him of something he had enjoyed earlier that he would not be seeing again.

He took a deep breath to fortify his resolve and looked her straight in the eye. 'I did not bring difficulty to your family, Miss Strickland. It was here long before I arrived.'

'But you are supposed to make it better,' she insisted. She was looking at him as though he could work miracles, again.

He fought the urge to play the gallant and come to her rescue. He was not required to do so. But how hard could it be to convince Charity to return to London? At the very least, he could try and fail. Either result would gain him an excuse to remain in Hope's company for a few more days, hoping that things between them might change.

More likely, it would end just as their last interaction had. She might seem devoted now, but all he was likely to get in reward was more heartache.

'I will pay you,' she blurted and he felt the euphoria deflate as their roles returned to the realm of the disappointingly understandable.

'*"I will pay you"* says the woman who has no money, without even enquiring as to my fee.' He shook his head. 'It explains much about how your family came to be in financial trouble.'

'I will find a way,' she said. 'Set your price and I will meet it. Anything you want, I will give it to you, if you will help me with my sister.'

His mind flew straight back to the place it should not go, full of innuendo and wild fantasy. He had half a mind to tell her what he truly wanted from her and announce that he was happy to discharge the duty now that they had settled on a price for it. But chances were, she would not even understand what he was saying.

Instead, he let out an exasperated sigh and said, 'Never mind. I shall add it to Mr Leggett's bill. Show me where to find her and I will haul her home.'

'The manor house is in Berkshire,' she said. 'I will leave a note for Grandmama and tell the servants that we are returning the items we have found. We will take the Comstock carriage.'

'*We?*'

'It might seem strange for you to go alone,' she said.

'Not really,' he assured her, already imagining what could happen if he had another opportunity to be alone with her.

'It would not be proper for you to be alone in the house with Charity,' she said.

He stared at her, searching for some proof that she saw the irony in her words. She was looking at him with the same sanctimonious disapproval that she had used on the first day they'd met.

He threw up his hands in surrender. 'Very well. We will go to Comstock Manor. Together. Tomorrow.'

'But…'

He held up a hand. 'You sister is most likely safe, for the moment. Since she is in the place she wished to be, I doubt she will take flight before tomorrow afternoon. And I have no intention of setting off, alone in a carriage with an unmarried woman, at nightfall. No matter how innocent you might think it, there is not a person in London that will not assume an elopement if we tear off into the night to-gether.'

She paused to consider, and blushed as she understood. Clearly, she had been thinking of him as a utility, rather than a warm-blooded man. Then she nodded in agreement. 'We will set off first thing tomorrow morning.'

'Very good,' he replied. They would have the whole thing settled by mid-afternoon and he would be back in London by night-fall, alone.

As usual, Hope's life seemed to be better the moment Gregory Drake arrived. It should not have been so. Her family was still horri-ble, the diamonds were still missing and the new Earl might appear at any moment. Still, she felt better.

There was also the fact that Mr Drake had been trying to escape her since the moment they had first kissed. She had insulted him multiple times and offended him in ways she could not fully understand. And yesterday, she might have, quite accidentally of course, sent him a note that implied she was languish-ing on a divan and awaiting his romantic at-tentions.

Yet he was going to help her. Whatever Mr Leggett was paying him could not possibly be enough. Though she could not help it, the fact that they would be trapped for hours in a carriage together gave her a thrill of joy. He had made it quite clear that he could handle retrieving the last item on their list without her help. When he had left the house yesterday afternoon, she might never have seen him again.

And yet? Here they were.

He'd arrived at her house this morning, at eight rather than ten, ready to set off for the manor. She noticed that he had not bothered to pack as much as a change of linen for the trip. It appeared he expected a return to London as soon as the matter was settled. Then he could go back to ignoring her, just as he'd been intending to.

Perhaps he wanted to return quickly, but that was not what she wanted, at all. She did not want to experience any more emergencies that required his help, nor did she intend to manufacture one. But it was horrible to think that he might slip away again with a bow, a smile and an invoice for services rendered.

It would be easier if she were anyone other than who she was. Charity or Grandmama

would have not hesitated to do something outlandish enough to hold his attention. But Hope
was supposed to be the proper one. So far, her
attempts at being daring and reckless with Mr
Drake had only seemed to make things worse.
Gregory, she reminded herself, as the carriage
rolled away from the town house and towards
the edge of the city. Before the day was out,
she must at least find an excuse to call him
by his name.

She had not bothered with a veil today, for,
with the family crest on the door of the carriage, it should not surprise people that she
was inside. But she made sure that all the
shades stayed down until they were well out
of the city, so that no one would realise that
she was travelling unchaperoned with a gentleman.

'You could have brought a maid,' Gregory
said, as she finally pulled back the curtain to
let in the light.

'There was no time,' she said firmly. If this
was the last time she was to see him, she had
not wanted Polly sitting between them to spoil
things.

'You found time to choose hair ribbons
to match your gown,' he said in a dry tone.

'And to pack a valise and write to your grand-mother.'

'I did not want witnesses,' she said. 'For Charity's sake,' she added, struggling for an explanation that was not too ridiculous. 'I do not need the maids gossiping about her fool-ishness.'

'Of course not,' he said. 'They will gossip about yours instead.'

'That is probably true,' she replied, surren-dering. 'It is about time, I think. Faith and I were the sensible ones in the family. Now that she is no longer watching me, it is much more difficult to behave than I thought it would be.'

He turned away suddenly, and she was sure it was to hide a smile. Then, without turning back, he said, 'I suspect it will be easier once the new Comstock has arrived and you no longer have to hare about London in a closed carriage with a stranger.'

'I am not sure what we are to each other, Mr Drake,' she replied. 'But we have not been strangers to each other for quite some time.'

'Only days,' he reminded her. 'It has been less than a week since we met.'

'And what has happened between us…'

she said cautiously. 'Would you describe it as normal?'

'No,' he said, much more quickly than she'd hoped he would.

He saw the shocked expression on her face and corrected himself. 'I mean, the activities are normal enough. If we were married, for example. Or...' he hesitated again '...or if we were in love. But never in my life... Well, not with a proper young lady, at least. And certainly not a proper young lady who I have only known for days.'

'Oh.' There had been a strange, vibrating sensation deep inside her, when he had said the word 'love'. It was rather like how she imagined a target felt when struck by an arrow. Until this moment, she had never thought of Cupid as anything other than a myth. But today, if she had looked out the window and seen him with bow in hand, she would not have been a bit surprised.

Her half of their interaction was suddenly much clearer. She was in love with Gregory Drake.

'Oh,' she repeated, nodding in understanding. It explained why she felt better each time she saw him and worse each time he left. It was why she couldn't seem to stop doing foolish things like kissing him when he came near to her. And why, even now, a part of her brain was searching for something she could do to make him stay.

And whatever it was would have to be spectacular, for it appeared that the feelings she had were not reciprocated. He had described love and marriage as a hypothetical explanation. But there was nothing in his tone or face to make her think he intended testing the hypothesis any time soon.

'And you barely know me,' he added, as if this was important.

'While you know me quite well,' she added. 'Whatever Mr Leggett has not told you could be found in *Debrett's*.'

She had said something wrong again. His expression had changed from open confusion to the distant smile he wore while working for her. 'You seem to think that being able to trace someone's family tree for generations is the same as knowing an individual. It is not, Miss Strickland. In fact, it is another thing entirely.'

At least, this time, she did not need Charity to explain how foolish she had been. 'I must apologise again, Mr Drake. I did not mean to imply that a person without such heritage is any less valuable. It is just that...' She bit her lip. 'Everything that happens in my family has happened to others. My father, my uncles and my grandfather have all *done* things. Although I am not proud of their actions, even my grandmother and Charity have stories to tell. While I... Well, I am simply not very interesting.'

Now he looked startled, as if the fact had never occurred to him, then blurted without hesitation, 'On the contrary, Miss Strickland, I find you fascinating.'

'Really?' She tried not to be too encouraged.

'You tell stories of physical altercations with your sisters that lead to dented pewter, cracked plaster and bloodshed.'

'All children are prone to mischief,' she said.

'You think a dismembered toe is a beloved childhood plaything.'

'Actually, it is a prosthetic,' she corrected.

'You steal inkwells from family friends.'

'Not usually. That was an aberration,' she said.

'And you kiss like an angel,' he concluded.

They both sat in silence for a moment, as if neither of them had expected such an open admission.

Then he went on as if it had not just happened. 'I have no such childhood stories to tell. Yours have been both entertaining and enlightening.'

She leaned forward. 'Now I can prove that we are definitely not strangers. I cannot think of another person outside my family that knows so much about me.' She frowned. 'But I still know very little about you. Would it be rude of me to enquire about your childhood? In the name of friendship, of course,' she added.

'In the name of friendship, I will speak of it,' he said, his natural smile returning. 'If you have spoken to your sister, you are aware that I never knew my parents.'

She nodded.

When she did not seem surprised, he went on. 'I was left on a farm in Essex without as much as a name to give me a clue to my past. The farmer chose Gregory from his father and Drake...' He paused.

'For Sir Francis Drake?' she questioned.

'For a male widgeon swimming in the duck

pond.' He paused again, as if waiting to see if she would laugh.

'It does not matter where it came from. It suits you well,' she said.

He nodded his thanks and continued. 'The farmer and his wife took me in because they had no children of their own. And for the money that had been provided for my care, of course. But they had no real affection for me, nor I for them. When I was old enough to do so, I was expected to work. I learned to weed a garden, clean a kitchen and milk a cow. I also learned that I had no desire to do any of them again, even if my life depended on it.'

'But clearly you were educated,' she said, surprised.

'At the village school run by the vicar,' he answered.

She could remember seeing such children in the schoolroom at the vicarage, struggling through lessons, just as her father had struggled to persuade their fathers of the need for at least a smattering of reading and mathematics.

'When I was old enough, a letter came from a solicitor in London that said I was to go to a proper school that would prepare me for university. I am sure the farmer only allowed it because he would be receiving no more money to keep me.'

'That is a blessing, I suppose,' she said, trying to imagine what it would be like if her grandmother and grandfather had viewed her not as family, but as something between a servant and a burden.

'It was difficult at first,' he admitted. 'The young gentlemen I met there had little patience for an ignorant country lad.' Then he smiled. 'Fortunately, I was strong for my age and a quick student.'

'What did you have an aptitude for?'

'Far too many things,' he said, with a laugh. 'But I had no real attraction for any of them. I considered law, the church and banking, only to reject them all.'

'And seeing how you reacted to the toe, I doubt you'd have made a good surgeon,' she added.

He winced. 'Nor an officer. I am not, by nature, a violent man.'

'And you do not like following orders,' she reminded him and received another nod.

'I lacked the patience to be a secretary or man of business, catering to every whim of some nobleman.'

'You sought independence,' she said.

'I wanted to come and go as I wished. To work or rest as the mood struck me. None of the professions I considered would allow for such freedom.'

'This explains what you did not want to do,' she agreed. 'But not how you chose what you did.'

'I matriculated from Cambridge without plans and with dwindling funds, so I went to London to seek my fortune. There, I happened upon an old school friend who was in need of a stiff drink and an understanding ear. It seems he had lost a considerable amount of money in a disreputable gaming hell and was afraid to tell his father. I offered to investigate the matter and found the faro table was rigged. When I returned his losses, he pressed a reward into my hand to guarantee my silence.'

'And you decided to make a job out of helping people?'

He shook his head. 'On the contrary, I refused to take his money. A friend does not expect payment when help is needed.' Then he smiled. 'But the men that saw me handle the matter at the gaming hell were strangers to me. One of them needed his younger brother rescued from an adventuress. Another needed an unwelcome houseguest removed. I helped them and they paid me to do it.'

'And they told others?'

He nodded. 'I have become quite popular. The income from other people's troubles has got me a rather nice house in Wimpole Street.'

'But that is just around the corner from our home.' She had imagined him maintaining simple bachelor's quarters somewhere, until he had mentioned his servants at the ball. She had never expected to find him living so close to the Comstock town house.

'It has been most convenient working for your family,' he said with a grin. 'I can help you in the morning and be home in time for tea. If any of your neighbours need my services, please be sure to recommend me to them.'

'Do you plan on continuing in your career for long?' It should not matter to her if his job allowed him enough income for a wife and family. But the longer she was with him, the more curious she became.

'Money is no longer my motivation, if that is what you are wondering,' he said. 'I mean to work as long as the job interests me.' Then he gave her a probing look. 'Solving one last, enormous task would be a wonderful way to end my career.'

'You are speaking of my problem,' she said quietly. 'The one I told you that you cannot help with.'

'You trust me with your sister's reputation and your own. But you keep hinting at a thing so big that I cannot manage it. It is clear to me that it troubles you.' He frowned for a moment, as if he could not quite understand his own curiosity. 'I do not like seeing you upset. Will you ever tell me what it is so that I may fix it for you?'

'You have a great deal of confidence in your own abilities,' she said.

'Of course I do,' he replied. 'I have never failed.' Then he gave her another of his half puzzled, half worried looks. 'But it is more than that. I appreciate the confidence you have shown in me, thus far. I do not want a secret to stand in the way of it.'

His eyes were soft again, as they had been when he had asked for her trust in the sitting room. It made her feel warm and safe, and a little sad that she could not give him what he wanted. 'And I do not want to be the person to destroy your perfect record by asking the impossible,' she said. 'I really do not think there is anything you can do for me. When we return to London, you will complete the list we gave you. I cannot expect more than that.'

'A Herculean task.' The smile he gave her now was the breathtaking one that he had given her on the first day. 'What use is my reputation if I baulk at doing the impossible?'

She wanted to tell him, almost as much as he wanted to hear it. She had told him before that it was a problem that could only be shared with Comstock. No matter what his temperament or marital state, the Earl was head of the family and was the only one who could decide what was to be done about the diamonds.

But suppose Mr Drake became part of the family? There would be no reason not to share her burden with a man who was her husband, or at very least her betrothed.

'I would be able to show you what I am facing when we arrive at the manor.'

He leaned forward, ready to aid her.

She held up a finger in warning. 'I would, if I wished to. But you have made it plain that you wish to be out of my life as soon as you have found the last item on the list. This is the sort of secret I cannot reveal to a man who refused to bring a clean shirt on this trip because he did not want to be trapped in the same house with me overnight.'

'You know my reasons for avoiding you,' he said, sounding almost as prim as she'd felt before meeting him.

'It is because you are afraid of what will happen,' she said, shaking her head. 'So am I. But unless we can overcome that fear, I cannot tell you what you want to know and you cannot help me.' Then, she summoned all the courage she had and smiled at him. 'If things change? Then we will see if you can perform miracles, Mr Drake. Or may I call you Gregory?'

Chapter Eleven

The house was both more and less than Gregory expected it to be. In the bones, it was the sort of grand English manor one could not help but stand in awe of. A conglomeration of styles, from Gothic to modern, it had been built and rebuilt until it stretched to forty rooms and was set on acres of park land with trout streams, rose gardens and herb knots.

But on closer examination, it was clearly in need of care. The slates on the roof were cracked, as were the paving stones at his feet. The gardens were not yet choked with weeds, but it was clear that the gardeners fought a losing battle in them.

Inside was no better. The staff was smaller than he would have expected for such a large house and many of the rooms they passed through were cold and dark, the furniture swathed in holland cloth. When he pulled the covers back, he was relieved to see that the appointments were in better condition than the things they had been retrieving.

But that raised the question that had been tickling at the back of his mind since they had located the candlesticks on the first day together. If she was short on funds, there were dozens of things that would have fetched more money than she had probably got. What had made the Dowager choose the items she had?

Hope Strickland walked him through the house, taking care to point out the bedchamber that would be allotted to him, should he stay the night, as well as the chambers that belonged to her and her sister. Was this intended as encouragement to act on his desires? Was she truly offering herself to him, should he be brave enough to accept her? Or was she a naïve girl who did not understand the consequences of her actions?

There was also the matter of the mysterious problem she would not explain. He wanted to help her. He wanted other things as well. To hear Hope Strickland call him by his name in a moment of passion, for instance.

There was a way to have that and his honour as well. He should settle the problem of Miss Charity, then catch the next mail coach back to London. Once there, he could wait for the return of the Dowager, or Leggett, or even the new Comstock so he might ask permission to offer for Miss Hope.

But in the time that took, she might change her mind about him. Literature was crowded with metaphors about striking hot irons and seeking forgiveness rather than permission. If he went to her room tonight and declared himself, by morning there would be only one course of action.

Had his father thought that, before bedding his mother, or had it always been his intention to leave her? And after the pain and isolation of his own childhood, what would possess him to risk the future of his wife and child by repeating his parents' mistake?

Now, Hope was looking at him with a smile that was both seductive and expectant. She knew what she wanted from him and was awaiting his answer.

He responded in the only way an honourable man could, with a blank look and an obtuse smile. 'This has been very informative.

But now I think it best that you take me to your sister.'

The further they got from the bedrooms, the more the old proper Miss Strickland returned. Her spine stiffened and her smile disappeared. Her sweet lips pursed into a frown. By the time they'd reached the library, she was in high dudgeon and stormed into the room, hands on hips to confront her sister. 'Charity, how could you?'

Miss Charity barely looked up from the pile of dusty journals that surrounded her. 'Quite easily, I assure you. I walked to the George and got my ticket for the eight o'clock coach…'

'You walked all the way to the George! At night and unescorted? Are you mad?'

The argument carried on without him, for Gregory had stopped on the threshold, momentarily stunned by the room. In his experience, people kept their libraries on the sunny side of the house to make best use of the available light when reading. But this had to be the darkest room he'd ever seen. It was full noon outside, but the frost-blasted ivy climbing the windows and the velvet curtains surrounding them left the room as dark as a crypt.

'I see you have brought Mr Drake with you to scold me as well,' Charity said, ignoring her sister's questions. 'Come in, Mr Drake. And the answer to your question is that it is better for the books.'

He started at being addressed, for he had said nothing to indicate the direction of his thoughts.

He was trying to frame the best response to her statement when she clarified it for him. 'You were standing on the threshold, staring at the windows, and I assumed you must be wondering why the room is so dark. It is because it has been designed with the comfort of the books in mind and not the readers. Too much light cracks the bindings and fades the ink.'

'I see,' he said, stepping into the room and joining the pair of sisters.

'We did not come all this way to admire the architecture,' Hope snapped. 'We have come to take you home.'

'Back to London, you mean,' Charity replied. 'Must I remind you that the town house is not my home any more than the manor is? At the moment, as you have been pointing out each time you hector me, we do not have a home. Nor did I have any money for alternate transportation.'

'You could have taken the Comstock equipage.'

'And left you and Grandmother with nothing? You'd have refused to allow it.'

'Ladies,' Gregory Drake said softly, holding his hands palm out to signal a stop to the conversation.

They both turned to look at him, a matching fire in their very different brown eyes.

He spoke to Hope in his most diplomatic tone, as if she were any other client and not the woman he wished to marry. 'Miss Strickland, need I remind you that you brought me here in hopes that I would mediate for you? I cannot do that if you wish to speak for yourself.'

She opened her mouth ready to retort, then snapped it shut again and shot another hot glare at her sister before turning back to him. 'Reason with her. It is plain that I cannot.'

When she made no move to leave, he added a conciliatory smile. 'It might be easier if you took this opportunity to refresh yourself from our journey. Then we might all meet again and discuss the matter over supper.' He had hoped to be gone by then. But if he wanted to settle the matter quickly, he had best give her some reason to co-operate.

Her jaw gave another involuntary snap and clench. Then it relaxed as it occurred to her that he had just promised to stay the night. She cast a final glare at Charity, then smiled at him. 'I shall see you both at eight. In the dining room,' she added, staring at her sister and the empty tea tray sitting on the table beside her. Then she quit the room.

There was a moment's silence after the door latch clicked shut. Then Charity looked up at him with a stubborn smile. 'Now, I suppose you shall call me an impertinent child and threaten to drag me back to London to do penance at Almack's for my misbehaviour.'

'The thought had crossed my mind,' he said. He looked at the chair beside her, calculated its probable level of discomfort when compared with everything else wrong in the room and then leaned a hip against a nearby library table. 'Save me the time and tell me if it will be effective.'

'No,' she said, with another smile.

'Then I shall have to try a different tack. I shall reason with you, as I would a man.'

'A truly novel approach,' she said with a surprised nod.

'I understand that you could not have asked for the family carriage, because you were sure the answer would be no.'

'You have met my sister. Do you doubt it?'

'But by leaving suddenly, you gave her unnecessary worry. That was quite unfair of you.'

There was a flash of something like contrition on the girl's face, before she said, 'Her refusal would have been unfair as well.'

He ignored her defence and went on. 'Apparently, she had reason to be concerned about you. You were safe enough on the mail coach. But it is dangerous of you to walk the streets at dusk alone. You may think that you are protected from robbery and assault by a plain face and a quick mind. But you aren't much more than seven stone soaking wet and there is no woman alive who is ugly enough to avoid unwanted attention from a certain type of ruffian.'

'I admit to my mistake,' she said. 'But at the time, I saw no other solution.'

'Then you did not look very hard,' he countered. 'Should you think of doing such a thing again, you will contact me and I will give you the money to hire a post chaise so you and your maid might ride in comfort and safety.'

'And then you would tell my sister what I have done, so she could put a stop to it,' Charity retorted.

'Not necessarily,' he said. 'If you asked for my word on the matter I would keep it, as long as I did not think you were doing anything too foolish or dangerous.' He glanced around the room and shook his head. 'While I cannot fathom why someone would be eager to sit in this room, I do not think your presence here puts you in any immediate risk.'

'My sister feels I have an unnatural attachment to the house,' she said.

'And do you?'

She thought for a moment. 'Despite what Hope might think, I understand that I cannot live here for ever and that I need to make plans for the future. She believes that I should do so by attending balls and throwing myself in the way of any eligible man who looks twice at me. I believe that the key to my future is in one of the books of this library.'

He waited for her to elaborate. When it was clear that she had no intention of doing so, he spoke. 'Then I see no reason why you cannot make your sister happy as well as yourself. If you wish to read the books, take a crate full of them back to London. When you are through with them, exchange them for another batch. Attend a few balls to placate your sister and spend the rest of the time in study.'

She looked surprised at the suggestion. Then she nodded. 'If that is all it takes to make her happy, I can abide by the conditions. Though there might still come a time when I need to return to the house.'

'When it does, you will approach me and I will arrange for your travel. Then we will both explain the trip to your sister.'

She looked surprised. 'That does seem to be a most rational solution.'

He held up a finger. 'I have but one condition.'

'Of course you do,' she said, crestfallen.

'We must put the plan into effect tomorrow. Or the day after, if that is how long it takes for you to gather your research. I promised your sister that I would bring you back to London and have no intention of breaking my word.'

Her eyes narrowed as she considered the plan.

'You agreed it was sensible just a moment ago,' he reminded her.

She sighed. 'Very well. We will return to

London tomorrow with as many books as the coach can hold.' Her eyes narrowed again. 'If you can get Hope to agree to the plan as well.'

'I am sure she will,' he said. 'I can be very persuasive, when it is necessary.'

'I expect you can,' she said, giving him a different sort of look entirely. 'Now, if that is all...' She glanced back at her books, then at the door, clearly eager to go back to her studies.

'Not quite,' he said, wondering how best to phrase the questions he needed to ask. 'You said that I should come to you when I could get no further.'

'I was under the impression that the completion of the entail was going quite well without any help from me,' she said, still watching him.

'You also said that was not my only task.'

She smiled. 'You are having troubles with my sister.' She steepled her fingers and leaned forward. 'Please, tell me more.'

'Do I have your word that you will not share this conversation with her?' he asked.

Charity laughed. 'You are still treating me as if I were a gentleman. How novel. I assure you, Mr Drake, I will say nothing.'

Now he was left with how to ask the questions he wanted answered. 'I do not fully understand your sister.' He thought for a moment. 'And I would very much like to. In fact, I must be sure I understand her completely before I proceed.'

'Does this pertain to the task Mr Leggett set for you of putting her off marrying the heir?' She was staring at him intently.

'Yes.' He thought for a moment. 'Somewhat.' And at last, he confessed. 'But it is also a personal matter.'

Now Charity's smile widened. 'I see.'

He took a breath. 'I want to know the reason for her obsession with Miles Strickland.'

'Then why are you asking me?'

'Because she has been loath to tell me. And before things progress any further...' God, had he actually said that? He must hope that, of all the things Miss Charity understood, they did not include how near he and her sister were to the point of no return.

He took a breath and tried again. 'Is she seeking a man with a title? Is it the rank that is important to her? Is it the money?'

'You want to know if another sort of man might have hope of marrying my sister?'

She paused, as if waiting to see how much

he was willing to admit. When he said nothing, she continued. 'She has, on at least one occasion, warned me against snobbery and suggests that I emulate our own parents' humble behaviour.'

'That is good to know,' he said, trying not to be too encouraged.

'Given our difficulties, neither of my sisters considered it possible to marry for love. Faith sought money, but Hope is more concerned with security. The new Earl is the only man she can think of who would give that to the whole family.'

'But if all three of you are both safe and financially secure?'

'And free from prosecution or censure for playing fast and loose with the entail,' Charity added.

'Of course,' he agreed.

'Then I should think she would be more concerned with her own happiness than my future,' Charity said. 'I have been awaiting that moment for as long as I can remember. And if you are wondering if I approve of you as a future brother-in-law...'

'I did not ask that,' he said hurriedly.

'The situation is purely hypothetical,' she

reminded him. 'If she did not feel the need to marry Comstock, I see no reason that she might marry an untitled gentleman as Faith did. Or even someone in trade, should she have affection for him. A man such as yourself, for instance. And now, if you will excuse me, I have much reading to finish before supper.'

Chapter Twelve

After she had been banished from the library, Hope found a maid to prepare the room for Mr Drake. Then she set about replacing the items that they had found in London. The candlesticks went to their place at the very centre of the long dining table where they provided light on the days when only the family was home to eat and good silver was not necessary.

The inkwell went on the left corner of the desk, for her grandfather had been left-handed. But suppose Miles Strickland favoured his right? Hope stared at it for a second, pondering the need for a move, and decided it would remain where it was. Anything else looked wrong to her.

The portrait required the help of the two footmen still at the manor. While Grandfather might have thought it belonged behind a door, it annoyed her to see the succession out of order. This required moving Comstocks numbers five to eight further down the gallery and pounding a new nail for Grandfather at the end of the row.

Once this was done, there was the matter of the oddment to sort out. She could not remember where it had been when they had first discovered it. After, its primary home had been the nursery. But that would take an excessive amount of time to explain to a new generation of Stricklands who might find it strange. Eventually, she decided on a shelf in the small parlour. Since that room also held the family Bible, she took the time to update the listing, explaining that it was no longer buried in the back garden without providing any embarrassing details on the reason for the exhumation.

At last, she paid a visit to the lock room to retrieve the false parure, then returned to her bedroom, as had been suggested, and sat wondering how much time should be allowed for the dust to settle on the argument that must be taking place in the library.

Charity did not like being dictated to and

flatly refused to be reasoned with. At any minute, she was likely to burst into Hope's room to inform her that she was under no obligation to listen to a stranger's opinion of where she should be spending her time.

The afternoon had passed in silence, which made Hope all the more nervous as she waited for the inevitable explosion. But as she'd requested, Charity had appeared at dinner, promptly at eight. They were hardly started on the soup course when she'd announced her intent to return to London as soon as she was able to collect her research sufficiently for travel.

Gregory Drake never ceased to amaze her. He had been able to do exactly what she'd asked of him in a single afternoon. And he'd had time afterwards to prepare for dinner. As usual, his suit and linen were immaculate. He had managed a shave and change of cravat, despite his refusal to pack for an extended stay. The man was not just a worker of miracles, he was a miracle himself. Once Charity retired to the library, as she always did after supper, the two of them could be alone and she could thank him.

He had ignored her hints in the hall, earlier. But it was not from a want of desire. What she had asked him to do was wrong. But for the first time in her life, she did not care.

There was still a part of her mind that knew it would be better for the family if she married Miles Strickland. But that part grew smaller by the minute. That same family that she'd wanted to help had been trying to talk her out of her plan for weeks. Nothing they'd said or done had persuaded her she was wrong.

And then Gregory Drake had kissed her. When he had lied about it at the ball, the idea that the Earl might be married had devastated her. But now, she prayed it was true. It had been much easier to plan for a life of sacrifice when she had not known what she would be giving up. Now, she could not imagine a future without Gregory in it.

If he refused to come to her, when they had retired for the evening, she would have to go to him. If she could not manage to tempt him with her body, she would tempt him with the secret he was obsessed with learning. This time, there would be no sudden angry departures. She would not let him escape her arms until she had heard a promise of marriage.

But before her happy future could begin, she had to get rid of her little sister. On any other night, Hope would have had trouble getting Charity to put down her books for a meal. But tonight she arrived at the table empty handed and was unusually loquacious. Afterwards, instead of disappearing to the library, she insisted that they adjourn to the parlour and set up the chessboard.

When Hope remarked that she was too tired from the journey to manage such a game, Charity had encouraged her to go straight to bed and invited Mr Drake to play the white. He accepted and they played in silence, while Hope sat alone by the fire, pretending to read.

Hope was not sure what he had said to her sister, but it seemed Gregory had made a conquest. It was either that or Charity had guessed her intent and decided to play chaperon. And it seemed that Gregory had seized on the opportunity as a way to protect her from herself and avoid another encounter like the one they'd had in the town-house library.

Why did he not understand that, for the first time in her life, she did not want to do the right and proper thing? Nor did she want to be saved from herself by well-meaning family. By half past ten, when the last of her patience had failed, she announced that it was time for bed.

Gregory rose, only to have Charity seize him by the wrist. 'If you are tired, Hope, then you must quit complaining about it and go to sleep. Goodnight to you. Another game, Mr Drake? I insist we make it two out of three.'

There was nothing for it but to retire as she had announced she was going to. She left quietly, with her dignity intact. It remained so until she had reached her room. Once there she threw herself on the bed and pounded the pillow in a girlish tantrum she was far too old for.

She had been unsure of what was happening while in London. She had known that she liked it. But for the sake of her reputation, she had known that she should not do it again. Gregory had agreed and was making an effort to stay separate from her. But rather than be grateful for his consideration, she was angry.

And jealous. Insanely so. Jealous of her own little sister, who had been showing both good sense and good manners, all evening. And who was, right this minute, alone with a man who did not belong to her.

If this was love, then she wondered why people were so eager to experience it, for it was very confusing.

She needed to talk to Gregory. More than talk. If there was something that made it impossible for a woman to marry any other man, then perhaps it worked the same way for men. If they did it, there would be no question that they belonged together, for ever.

She called for a maid to help her out of her clothing and into a fresh nightgown. Then she dismissed the girl and sat quietly in the dark on the edge of her bed, with the door to the hall open a crack, listening. The house grew quiet, and quieter still. And then she heard footsteps in the hall, and the sound of the maid coming to her sister's room and leaving it again.

A little later, she heard masculine steps walking to the room that had been set aside for Gregory Drake. How long did it take a man to prepare for bed? She was not sure. She waited another fifteen minutes, listening for the faint chimes of the long-case clock in the hall and hoping for the sound of stockinged feet walking from his room to hers. When they did not come, she surrendered to her desires and crept down the hall to find him.

She paused at his door for a moment, unsure of what to do next. Did one knock before seducing a gentleman, or simply open the door? If he didn't want her, he would refuse. It would be embarrassing, but then, at least, she would know.

But he was not going to refuse her. She remembered the things he had whispered he could do to her and the things he wanted her to do to him. All that was waiting for her on the other side of the door.

She dropped her hand to the handle, worrying for just a moment that it might be locked, before feeling it turn easily. The door opened without a squeak and she thanked the Lord for the diligence of the servants in keeping the hinges oiled. Then she stepped through it and closed it quickly behind her.

The room was lit by a single bedside candle. He sat up in bed, his chest bare, the covers bunched at his waist. He had been reading. But now the book in his lap was forgotten. He stared at her as if waiting for an explanation.

For the moment, she had none. Her mouth had gone dry at the sight of all that smooth skin covering a fascinating array of muscles. She'd imagined what he must look like, under his clothes, but the reality was far more affecting than she'd imagined it would be.

'I thought you had gone to bed,' he said. His tone was matter of fact.

He had spoken to her many times. He'd even whispered honey into her ears. But until now, she had never noticed how beautiful his voice was, like the deep tolling of a bell in a valley.

'Hope?' Now he sounded concerned.

She wanted to tell him that there was no reason to worry. She was fine. In fact, she was better than she had ever been in her life, because she was with him. And something wonderful was about to happen. She was going to tell him exactly how she felt, if only she could manage to catch her breath.

Suddenly, she was on the floor, looking up at the ceiling. Gregory Drake was standing over her with a worried look on his face. Then he was crouching, his arm beneath her head, urging her to drink something from a flask in his hand.

She sputtered over her first sip of brandy.

'You fainted,' he said gently. 'Drink. When

you are feeling a little better, I will ring for a maid. Or perhaps your sister.'

'No!' At last, she'd found her voice. Apparently, it startled him for she could feel the slight jerk of his arm. She smiled hopefully up at him and reached out to touch the hand that held the flask. 'You do not want Charity to come here, do you?'

'Charity? God, no.' Now, he was the one to look faint. 'I have seen quite enough of your sister for one night.' He took the flask away, raised it to his lips and took a long, fortifying drink before answering. 'And if you are expecting a liaison, I am the one who should be creeping into your room.' He smiled.

'Am I doing it wrong?' she asked, still not sure exactly what *it* was.

'The whole situation is wrong,' he replied. 'I should not even know the location of your room and there are a hundred reasons why I should send you back to it.'

He stared down at the unbuttoned neck of her nightgown. 'But, damn me, when I look at you I cannot seem to think of any of them.'

'I am glad,' she said, straining up to kiss him before he could clear his head. He tasted of brandy and his mouth was open wide in surprise.

There was a moment where he still resisted. But only a moment. Then, he took control, cupping the back of her neck and holding her mouth to his and possessing it. It was every bit as shocking as the first kiss had been when she'd had the feeling that his iron self-control had slipped, giving her a glimpse of something wild and dangerous beneath it.

And so it seemed tonight. His other hand was unbuttoning the rest of her nightgown, pushing the fabric out of the way so he could reach her bare breasts. She trembled as his fingers touched her nipples, stroking lightly over their tips before closing a hand over one, warming it with his palm.

As his hand moved, the sensation rushed through her body and she arched her back and clenched her legs together. She struggled free of his kiss and turned her head into his naked shoulder, licking against the skin before grazing it with her teeth.

'You learn quickly,' he whispered, pushing her away. 'Show me what you want.' She wanted what he had promised her before, to be kissed until she begged. He moved against her mouth and she kissed the planes of his face, the sharp line of his jaw, the cords of his throat and the muscles of his chest. Then she felt the rough, flat nipple touch her lower lip. She seized upon it, trying to take it into her mouth, circling it with her tongue and biting gently.

But he did not beg, he laughed. 'Very well.' Now his mouth was on her breasts, repeating what she had done. Had it felt this way for him? She could not beg for it, because the sensation was beyond words. She squirmed under him, then relaxed, letting her legs open wide until he was laying between them.

As she moved, the sheet he'd wrapped about his waist shifted lower and she was surprised to feel nothing but bare skin rubbing against her thigh. Was it really possible that he had been lying in bed, wearing nothing at all?

She could not resist her curiosity and drew her knee up, then slid it down along his body, pushing the linen down with it. There was nothing but skin roughened by hair, as far as she could reach.

He seemed surprised by her explorations and grinned at her. Then he braced himself on his arms and slid back up her body, until they lay hip to hip.

She gasped.

He grinned and kissed her, teasing the inside of her mouth with his tongue, sliding in and out with a series of deep thrusts, as his manhood settled between her legs. 'Perhaps you would be more comfortable if we moved to the bed.' He kissed her breasts again, with long, slow pulls on her nipples.

'Here. Now. Please.' He was right. He had made her beg.

He paused again, surprised. 'Do you know what you are asking for?'

'No,' she admitted, on another gasp. 'Tell me.' She rubbed her leg against his again. He groaned and bucked once against her as she raised her hips to meet him.

His hands circled her waist to hold her still. Then he reached between them and stroked once between her legs, making her moan in surprise. 'I could pleasure you as we did in the drawing room, but I do not know that I will be able to stop at that.'

'Why?' she whispered.

'Because I would be forgoing a pleasure as great as the one you experience.' His hand moved lower and his fingers disappeared inside her. 'I will feel it when I take you as a man takes his wife, by spilling my seed inside you. There will be no turning back once we start and no time for regrets. Also, it will probably hurt.'

She had not expected there would be pain.

He dropped a gentle kiss on the open 'Oh' of her mouth. 'That is just the first time. After that, there will be nothing but pleasure, I swear on my life. But once that has been done, there can be no more secrets between us and no talk of marrying other men. You must tell me everything in your heart and your mind, and promise to love me, and only me, for the rest of your life.'

If simple desire had not been enough to convince her, his words were more than enough. Brief pain in exchange for someone to share her heart and soul with, not just for now but always. 'Yes,' she said, breathless and a little frightened. Then she tugged at the hem of her nightgown, pulling it up between them and over her head.

He released a hiss of breath from between his clenched teeth. 'Your body feels as I knew you would, like the reward of heaven itself.'

His lips roved down her throat and returned to her breasts. He buried his face between them and worshipped them with his tongue, his teeth and his hands.

The contact left her light-headed, as if she was floating in the same paradise he had imagined. She reached up and swept her hair forward, draping it over his shoulders.

He lifted his head and smiled. Then he slid down her body to kiss her between the legs as he had on the mouth.

Her first response was to pull away in shock. But his hands on her waist pulled her back again. At the renewed contact, a jolt of pleasure lanced through her body. She stiffened and then relaxed again, allowing him to do as he wished with her. She was rewarded with another pulse, and another, until the throbbing between her legs overwhelmed her.

Her fingers dug into the rug beneath her and she closed her eyes and arched her back. His fingers were pushing inside her again, spreading her wetness, stretching her. Then she felt the full weight of his body on hers and the sudden pain of his first thrust.

And afterwards, stillness, as his fingers stroked her until the pleasure grew in her again. She grabbed his biceps, feeling the taut muscle bunching under her fingers as he began to move. Her body seemed to cling to the unfamiliar fullness inside, tightening on it to heighten the sensation as he withdrew, only to enter again.

She could hear his measured breaths against her temple as he struggled for calm, waiting for her. But she did not want him calm. She wanted to break though the reserve and know that he was as helpless for her as she was for him. She dared to open her eyes and look up into his. She whispered his name.

His stroke faltered, and returned, stronger than before.

This time she said it louder. 'Gregory.' She gave herself over to the rhythm he set, rocking in time with him, letting her hands roam over his body. Everything about him was strange and wonderful, flat where she was curved and hard where she was soft. And where it mattered most he fit like a piece of herself she had never known was missing.

He was whispering to her, demanding that she come with him, as if they were on some journey that he did not want to complete alone. His breaths were ragged now, his movements a shuddering syncopation that made her body tighten and pulse against his. Then she felt a change. He muttered what sounded like a prayer and surged forward. Her body clenched. They were shaking in a rush of pleasure that went on and on until they were both exhausted.

They collapsed, him on top of her and her flat on the floor, staring up at the ceiling. When his head rose, his cheeks were flushed and his blond hair fell forward on to his face.

She reached up to smooth it. 'This is the first time I have seen you discomposed,' she said, smiling.

'Because you have bewitched me,' he said, with a happy sigh.

'Me?' She could not help being pleased with herself.

'Since the first day,' he said. 'It has been a losing struggle to keep my head.'

'If this is what happens when you fail, perhaps you should not try so very hard,' she said.

He pulled out of her and she sighed at the loss. Then he rose and scooped her up, carrying her across the room.

'What are you doing?' she said, laughing.

'What I should have done, before,' he said, with a stern look. 'I am taking you to my bed, where you belong.' He tossed her on to the mattress, then stood over her, hands on hips like a sultan surveying his conquest.

She stared for a moment, admiring the body she had felt rather than seen. Then she shook her head, to remove the fantasies forming there, and sat up. 'We cannot.'

'No?' He looked both surprised and disappointed. It was quite flattering.

She smiled. 'You said there could be no more secrets between us. Before we go any further, I must tell you the whole of our troubles. Then we will see if you are truly as brilliant as you claim to be.'

Chapter Thirteen

As she led him down the hall towards the Countess's suite, Gregory walked behind her, admiring the view. She was barefoot and naked, except for her rumpled nightgown, open at the throat so it hung low and bared her shoulders. Her hair was tousled and her skin was flushed. She looked well and thoroughly loved.

She looked back at him, smiled and held a finger to her lips, reminding him of the need for silence as they passed her sister's room.

He did not want to be quiet. He wanted to shout for joy. And to call a 'thank you' to her sleeping sister. When Hope had left them alone to play chess he had wanted to retire as well. Considering how much trouble he had caused by being alone with one sister, he dared not risk the reputation of a second one, even if their interaction was completely innocent.

But the younger Strickland had detained him, demanding one more game. The moment her sister was out of earshot she pushed away from the board. 'Now we will wait. Twenty minutes should be enough.'

'For what?' he had asked.

'For my sister to become angry enough to do something rash,' she said, with a smile.

He frowned at her. 'I do not want your sister to do something rash. And I do not need your help in winning her, if that is what you think you are doing.'

She laughed. 'Perhaps you need no assistance. But my sister needs twenty minutes.'

At last, he had relented. 'Twenty minutes, or twenty days. It should not matter either way, because nothing is going to happen between us until I have spoken with your grandmother.' It was pure luck that had made him say *nothing,* rather than *nothing more*. Even though she did not seem to try, Miss Charity was far too good at ferreting out secrets.

She was good at judging her sister's character as well. Though Hope had always claimed to be the proper one, he'd seen no evidence of it tonight. But it was no longer as important to protect her innocence as it had been. Before they'd made love, he had got a promise of devotion from her. There would be no more talk of the Earl, because she had promised to love only him.

He was going to marry Hope Strickland. The acceptance of his official offer was a foregone conclusion. Even so, he would make one, on one knee with a ring worthy of a daughter of one of England's noblest families. Tradition was important to her. It should be so to him as well. After all, he was starting a family line of his own. She would be the first Mrs Drake. There would be children. Offspring. Progeny. Descendants.

He thought he had been happy before. But now, his throat closed with emotion at the thought of the future. There had been an emptiness in him for as long as he could remember. And now Hope Strickland had filled it.

Ahead of him, she had stopped. She stood at the Countess's open bedroom door, beckoning him to enter. When they were both inside, she shut it tightly and lit the candles on the bedside table from the one she'd carried. 'What I am about to show you might be hard to see in candlelight. But I think that was rather the point all along. A dark room hides a multitude of sins.'

He felt a sudden chill of foreboding. Had that been a reference to what they had just done, or was she speaking of something else?

She continued speaking, unaware. 'I removed these from the lock room this afternoon, while you were busy with Charity.' She pulled a velvet box from the dresser and spilled the contents on to the bed.

'The Comstock diamonds,' he said, surprised.

Now she was poking through some of the most famous jewels outside the royal family as if they were nothing but jumble.

'The full parure consists of a tiara, eardrops, two rings, a brooch. And, of course, the lavalier, which must be three carats at least. Grandmama rarely wears anything more than the smaller of the rings. She has complained for as long as I can remember that the rest are too heavy for any occasion less than a visit to court.'

As he stared at the jewels, the reason for her secrecy came clear. To verify what he already knew, he picked up the necklace, weighted it in his hand for a moment, then blew on it, holding it up in the candlelight to check the surface for fog.

Then he set it down with a sigh. 'How long since the real stones were replaced with paste?'

'I have no idea,' she said, sitting on the edge of the bed and tucking her feet beneath her to keep them warm. 'It was hard enough getting Grandmama to describe the rest of the items she took. But when she did not mention them, I became suspicious and examined them.' She ran a fingernail along the surface of one of the larger stones. 'They are scratched. No true diamond would have such damage.'

'And you asked her what had become of them?'

'She flatly refuses to say a word about them, claiming she will explain it all to the new Comstock when he arrives.' She waved a hand at the jewellery beside her and laughed bitterly. 'What will she say to him that might matter? A theft of this magnitude cannot just be explained away.'

'You were planning to give yourself to the Earl,' he said, shocked, but not surprised.

She cocked her head to the side, looking

up at him with a smile that had become wiser in the last hour. 'I did not think of it in that way. I was not planning to *give* anything but my hand. But that was not what he actually would have wanted from me.' She looked into his eyes and one part of him melted as another grew hard. 'I may have diminished my value somewhat, since meeting you.'

'You most certainly have not,' he said. 'You were worth more than a pile of cold stones when we began. And now? I would not trade a minute with you for all the jewels in England.'

'Thank you,' she said. 'But much as I like to hear them, your beautiful words will not solve my problem.' She patted the bed beside her, indicating that he should sit. 'I need your beautiful brain to do that. Or at least Mr Leggett's beautiful money. How much has he given you to sort our problems?'

'He said I could have what was needed,' Gregory said, collapsing prone on the bed next to where she sat. 'I was to spare no expense.'

'Ha.' She made a sound that was far too harsh to call a laugh and fell back to lay at his side. 'And how much have you spent so far?'

'Seventy-seven pounds, five shillings and sixpence,' he said.

'That is very precise,' she said, glumly.

'I have receipts,' he said. 'I would not be in demand if I were not so accurate. I will waive my fee to him, of course, since we are to be family.'

'Are we?' she said, rolling to face him.

'That will be up to his wife's younger sister.' He took her hand and kissed the knuckles. 'I plan to speak to your grandmother the moment we return to London and hope that I shall claim a connection to Mr Leggett before he has even come back from Italy.'

'Do you think he might give us a wedding gift of fifty thousand pounds?' She reached to the jewels at her side and perched the tiara awkwardly on her forehead. 'Or perhaps one hundred and fifty,' she said, with a regal wave of her hand. 'You are far better at guessing the value than I. But I guess that the diamonds must be worth at least that.'

'You are assuming we could buy them back,' he reminded her. 'I doubt the biggest stone remains uncut. There will be no equal to be found, even if we could afford it.'

'At least we still have the settings.' She sighed. 'Although, with the luck I've had, I would not be surprised to scratch the surface and find they are gilded tin.'

'But at least this restores my faith in your grandmother's sanity,' he said, staring up at the canopy above the Dowager's bed. 'I was wondering why she sold such rubbish to get by. If she had already run through the money for the diamonds, it makes more sense.' He stopped, confused. There was something wrong in that assumption as well, but he was too tired to see what it was.

'It would have made even more sense, in the eyes of the law, if she had sold things that actually belonged to her.' Hope gave a bitter laugh. 'The rest of the jewels in her jewel case are real and not entailed. When I asked her why she did not part with those, she told me that they were gifts from Grandfather and had sentimental value.'

'Of course,' he said weakly.

'And now you see why I thought it was hopeless to even tell you. With your help, we have been able to replace the least important items. But I doubt that the Earl will be impressed by our efforts once he learns what is still lost.'

'That is quite possibly true.' And now he

could see why she had not wanted to tell him
of the problem, for he could not think of a
better solution than the one she had been considering.

'Have you heard anything more about his
arrival? How long do we have before he learns
what Grandmama has done?'

'No,' he admitted. Strickland was already
overdue. At best, they had a few weeks before the reckoning she had feared. Now that
she'd told him the whole truth, it appeared
she had been right all along. For a wrong of
this magnitude, marriage would have been
a reasonable way to heal the breach and re-
unite the two branches of the family. If it had
been any other woman, he'd have brokered
the match himself.

Instead, he'd made bold promises about
solving any problem put to him. He'd lain with
her and ruined the best chance she had for the
security she craved. Now the only thing he
could do to set things right was to produce
a king's ransom in diamonds on short notice
and out of thin air.

She poked him again. 'You have not fallen
asleep, have you?'

'No. Merely thinking.'

'You had gone so quiet, I was beginning to wonder. Do you have a plan?'

'The beginnings of one.' He was lying to her again. He had no idea what to do, other than stall and pray. 'Is the jewel case here? I wish to examine it.'

She rose on one elbow and gave him an odd look, then pointed to it, sitting on the mattress, a few inches from his head.

'Silly of me,' he said with a shrug and reached for it. 'It seems I have eyes for nothing but you.' Now that he'd started lying he could not tell one truth in twenty.

'I don't know what good it will do,' she said. 'He will not be impressed by a nice package if the jewellery is false.'

'It might do no good at all, but I must be thorough. I will not leave any avenues unsearched or any clues unexamined.'

'You cannot possibly think there is anything to be done,' she said, smiling in surprise.

He smiled back at her and felt the energy surging in his blood at the sight of such a supremely beautiful, infinitely desirable woman staring at him as if she thought he could hang the moon. She had confidence in him. He must have it as well. 'I solve problems. If I turn away when presented with a challenge, then what good am I?'

'If you can retrieve the diamonds, then you are not a problem solver, Mr Gregory Drake. You are a worker of miracles.'

He took a deep breath and felt more than his courage begin to rise. 'If that is what you require of me, Miss Strickland, I shall endeavour to provide.'

'That is not all I want.' She sat up and stripped her nightgown over her head, then straightened the Comstock tiara in her chestnut hair and added the massive, paste pendant which swung to hang between her magnificent breasts. Then, naked and bejewelled and as bold as a pagan princess, she straddled him.

If her body was not enough to make him forget his impending doom, her next words were.

'Take me, Mr Drake. Repeatedly. Until dawn.'

'Consider it done, Miss Strickland.'

Chapter Fourteen

Hope had never been the one to break rules.
If questioned, either of her sisters would have
declared her the one least likely to disobey
and most likely to tattle on those who did. But
after last night, she had to admit that being
good was not nearly as much fun as being bad.

Lying with a man before marriage was
something that a nice girl should never do.
But not only had she done it, she'd learned
that there was more to it than just lying still.
In fact, sometimes she had done no lying at
all. One could do things that were very improper while sitting, or standing, or kneeling
on a mattress and clinging tightly to the bed-
post while the man behind her whispered un-
speakable suggestions in her ear.

Worse yet, she had done those things in a

bed that was not hers, with the pride of the Comstock entail thumping furiously against her naked breasts. It was almost a relief to know the stones were paste, for she would have been afraid to do the things she'd done while wearing nothing but a small fortune in diamonds.

And she would do it all again, the minute she could get Gregory Drake alone. It was a shame that the object of the trip had been to collect Charity and take her back to London. If her sister had not been here, Hope might have made up some spurious excuse about beginning the inventory of the house. Then they might spend the week together, alone.

Of course, there would be no hope of finding the diamonds if they stayed at the manor. She did not think it would be possible for Gregory to figure out where they had gone, but she would enjoy seeing him try.

She came down to the breakfast table to find Charity already seated, a book spread on the table between her cup and her plate. Normally, she would have lectured her sister about reading at the table, but it was far too nice a morning to fret over trivialities. She took the chocolate pot and toast rack from in front of her sister, who did not even bother to look up from her work, and served herself.

'Good morning, Charity,' she said. When her sister said nothing, she answered for her. 'Good morning to you, Hope. Did you sleep well?'

Charity held up a finger to indicate that she was almost done with the passage she was reading. Then she slipped a ribbon between the pages as a marker and closed the book. 'I can speak for myself, thank you. Good morning, Hope. Did you sleep we...?' She'd looked up, the word trailing off into empty air. 'Well, well, well.' She cleared her throat. 'I mean, did you sleep well?'

The question was innocent, but the look on her face was anything but.

'Yes,' Hope replied, suddenly afraid to say anything more.

'That is good to know. And how did Mr Drake sleep?' Charity asked, with an arch look.

'You will have to ask him that. Or don't. Please,' she said. As usual, Charity knew more than she should. Was there something in her face that gave it all away? Was there some sort of brand that had appeared on her forehead to signal to the world that she had forbidden knowledge?

'Do not worry so, Hope.' Her sister held her cup out to be refilled. 'You look exceptionally well rested this morning.'

'Oh.' It was some consolation to know that the patronesses at Almack's would not bar the door against a fallen woman, should she have reason to return there. But it did not make this moment any easier.

And now the morning would be even worse. The door to the breakfast room opened and Mr Drake entered. He offered a respectful bow to her and a smile to Charity. He looked as he always did, deliciously perfect. Even with no valet, his suit was freshly brushed and his cheeks clean shaven. The gloves peeking out of his coat pocket were immaculate. 'I have been speaking with the coachman. He will be ready to depart at our convenience.' He was much better at hiding the activities of the previous night than she. There was nothing in his face or his posture to indicate that he'd gone to sleep with the rising of the sun, or spent time in a bed other than his own.

Charity smiled back at him with none of the sly awareness that she had used on Hope and offered him a plate of buns and teapot. 'Thank you so much for your help in this matter. The box is almost prepared. It should not take more than a few minutes once we are ready. Shall we say, twenty minutes?'

The perfectly composed Gregory Drake choked on his toast. It took a sharp slap on the back from Charity and half a pot of tea before he was able to catch his breath and answer, 'There is no reason to rush. I will call for the carriage at one.'

'And I will arrange for the kitchen to prepare a hamper so we might take tea on the road. Country air always gives me an appetite.'

At this, the poor man went pale, as if the mention of hunger put him in mind of something that had nothing to do with food.

'That is an excellent idea,' Hope said, glaring at her sister. 'Now perhaps you would like to go back to your book. We do not wish to keep you from your studies.' The sooner they were free of Charity, the better. The family had long since accepted that the youngest sister was the smartest one. But it sometimes felt like they were mice in a cage, the victims of her insatiable curiosity rather than the beneficiaries.

Before her sister could retort, there was a commotion in the front hall. Hope could hear her grandmother greeting the servants and calling for her luggage to be brought in from the carriage. Even more unexpected than that, the activity was accompanied by a flurry of high-pitched barking.

Then the Dowager appeared in the doorway. She was wearing a new travelling gown and had a small black and white dog tucked under her arm that yipped continually as he tried to wriggle free of her.

Gregory sprang to his feet in a show of respect, but the Dowager waved him back into his chair with her free arm. 'Please sit, Mr Drake. I am the one interrupting your breakfast. I have been in a rented carriage five long hours and my legs need a good stretch.'

She stared at her granddaughters. 'Of course, I would not have needed a post-chaise if the Comstock carriage had been available.'

'I am sorry, Grandmama,' Hope began. 'But Charity...'

'I read your note,' she said with a firm smile. 'I was impressed by your ability to single-handedly deal with an emergency that occurred during a time when I was not home to accompany you.' There was something in her eyes that said she had calculated the time-line to the minute and knew full well that the problem had been discovered long before they had set out and solved long before breakfast.

The dog let out another miserable whine and the Dowager signalled the footman hovering in the doorway. 'Take care of Pepper, Jenks. I am sure he would like to stretch his legs as well. One of them, at least. Once he is done, you are to bring him straight back into the house. He will be living here, now, and must get used to behaving inside.'

'Grandmama,' Hope said, with a warning tone. 'He cannot be coming to live here because we are not sure how long we will be staying.'

'Do not be ridiculous, Hope. Pepper can stay as long as he wishes.' Her grandmother smiled. 'He does not belong to me, you see.'

'You have no right to bring a strange dog into the place. Does it belong to your sick cousin?' Hope threw her hands in the air. 'I do not understand.' It was bad that Charity had returned, but now the whole family was back where they did not belong and had grown by one.

The Dowager stared at her as if she were being unforgivably dense. 'Have you not guessed what has happened? Did you not realise why I had gone to Bristol? The seas were rough. The poor fellow has not had a decent meal in weeks and kept down little of the food he did get. He needed time to recover before travelling on to London.'

'Your cousin is...' Hope raised her eyebrows. 'That cousin?'

'When I returned to London and found that you were both gone, I did not want to waste the time on a letter. The news is so amazing.'

There was a sound of distant barking and then the sudden yip of a dog that had attempted to chase something more inclined to fight than run.

The Dowager gave a worried look out the window. 'I hope Jenks has not let Pepper too near the stable cats. The Earl wanted someone to bring the little fellow to his new home and I volunteered. I am assured that he is normally a sweet-tempered creature. Pepper, that is, not the Earl.'

She smiled. 'But Miles is a sweet-tempered

creature as well. The pair of them have been cooped up in a small cabin for weeks. A dog needs to feel grass under his feet and there did not seem to be enough of it in London to suit him.'

'Miles?' Hope had heard but one in ten of the torrent of words in her grandmother's rambling discourse. But she had understood enough to realise that they had run out of time. She could not seem to take a breath. It was as if all the air was pushed out of her lungs, leaving her nothing to respond with. 'You saw him?'

'I escorted him back to London, where he will be for some time.' She gave the girls a disapproving look. 'I should never have given you such free use of the carriage, for he should be riding in it when he goes to the palace. Although he said it was not necessary to stand on ceremony. At least not until the formalities have been dealt with. There is a need to prove his identity, beyond doubt. Then there will be a Letter of Patent to transfer lands and title.' The Dowager waved her hand. 'It is all very tedious. Especially for Pepper, who did not like the town house at all.'

'Never mind the dog.' Now that she could

manage to get a word in, Hope had to struggle to keep from shouting. 'Tell me about the Earl.'

Her grandmother waggled a finger at her. 'You are not still thinking of him, are you? It is very shallow of you to throw Mr Drake aside before even meeting your cousin.'

She turned to Gregory with a somewhat sterner smile. 'The two of you will be marrying, of course. After what happened last night, I expect you will want to do so as soon as possible.'

'What happened?' Hope said, trying to sound as though she did not know the answer to the question.

Her grandmother frowned and shook her head. 'Lord save me from poor liars and silly young girls.'

Was there no way to hide the truth of her behaviour, even for a moment? Charity had been lying when she'd said that the change in her was not that noticeable. It explained why girls were taught to protect their innocence at all costs. But like many strict rules, obedience had been more important than understanding. Of all the things Gregory had taught her last night, why had he not explained that there could be no turning back because, once she returned to London, everyone would know exactly what she had done?

Worst of all, Grandmama was not her usual, flippant self. She was more stern than Hope had ever seen her and, rather than telling an amusing anecdote about her misspent youth, she was giving them both dark looks and talking of marriage as a *fait accompli*.

'Nothing of interest happened last night,' Hope blurted. Gregory's mouth, which had opened to speak, closed with a frown.

She continued. 'Charity can assure you of that, for I retired early and the two of them stayed up until all hours, playing chess. And I am not throwing anyone over for my American cousin, who is probably too old for me and married.'

'Old and married?' Her grandmother released a silvery laugh. 'Whatever gave you such an idea?'

'You, Charity and everyone else in the family,' she replied. 'Perhaps I have finally accepted what the two of you have been telling me all along. It would be too great a miracle for him to be young and unmarried. It is far more likely that he is old and has a wife and several children.'

'Then miracles do happen,' her grandmother said, stepping forward to pat her on the shoulder. 'He is barely thirty and single. He has nothing but Pepper to claim as family. Even now, the Crown is impressing on him his responsibilities and the need for an heir.'

'But I would never assume a man was right for me without even meeting him,' Hope said, staring down into her plate and trying to contemplate the magnitude of the mistake she had made. 'He might be miserly and foul tempered,' she added. 'He might not care about our family at all.' He might not be the sort of man she could love as she'd thought she loved the silent Gregory Drake.

'On the contrary, he is the kindest gentleman in the world.' Her grandmother was near to simpering over the newly arrived Comstock, who was, apparently, exactly the man Hope had expected him to be. 'Miles greeted me as long-lost family and expressed his intent to see that there is a settlement in place for the repair of the dower house and my expenses. I took the liberty...' She spun to display her new gown.

'You went shopping with his money,' Hope said with a sigh.

'He encouraged me to do it. He is writing a letter this very afternoon to thank Mr Leggett for his help in settling the family. And he enquired after you and your little sister. He did not say as much, but I am sure he means to see the both of you are well settled.'

'He does?' Her plan might not have been wise, but it had not been hopeless at all. Instead, she had abandoned it and thrown herself away on a man who did not want her until she had all but forced herself upon him.

'I think he was asking about you girls with a particular reason in mind.' Her grandmother giggled again. 'It is too late for you, Hope. But perhaps Charity...'

'Do not involve me in your schemes,' Charity said, without looking up from her book. 'I have no intention of marrying a man I have not met. And any man I do want to marry will have to fit certain criteria before I consider him a suitable husband.'

'He is young, rich and an earl,' the Dowager said. 'How much more can you expect from him?'

'Stop!' Hope rose so quickly that her chair

tipped backward, hitting the carpet with a thud that echoed her word. Her napkin, still clutched in her hand, waved like a flag of surrender as she pointed to the shocked faces around the table. 'Stop it this instant, both of you.' She turned to Charity. 'Not another word of this nonsense about standards so high that a peer will not suffice. If he offers, you will marry him and that will be that.' Then she turned to her grandmother. 'And not as much as a breath about it being *too late* for me.'

'But I assumed that you and Mr Drake...'

'You assumed incorrectly,' she said, glaring across the table at the man who had let her ruin herself. 'Mr Drake is nothing to me. And I am nothing to him. Once he has finished his job for our family, I never want to see him again.' She narrowed her eyes. 'If he were in any way decent, he would be gone already.' Then she threw her napkin to the ground and ran from the room.

Was he a fool or a coward? Gregory could not decide how to explain what had just happened to him. He'd sat in silence and let Hope do all the talking, amazed that she was so quick to deny him. After swearing there would be no one but him, it had taken one censorious glare from her grandmother to turn her mind and her future back to a marriage with her cousin.

Now that she was gone, the room fell silent. Charity returned to her book as if nothing had happened. The Dowager stepped forward and took an empty seat at the head of the table. At a glance in the direction of Jenks, the footman, a cup and plate appeared in front of her. Tea was poured and food offered.

She sipped, then looked over the rim of her cup at Gregory. 'Young man, I must know one thing before I decide what to do with you. You will answer in honesty. I will know if you do not.' She stared at him.

He nodded.

'Did you break her heart intentionally, or was it accidental?'

Charity looked up from her book. 'Grandmama, he—'

'I did not ask your opinion, girl.'

He gave her a brief nod of thanks, then turned to the Dowager. 'If I hurt her, it was without intent. Since we met...' How could he explain what had happened when he did not understand it himself? 'I have not been myself.'

'And who are you, when you are at home?' the old woman asked with the glare of a countess addressing someone of insignificance.

'Before I met your granddaughter, I thought myself a man of honour, good sense and moderation,' he admitted.

'And since?'

'I have been both better and worse than I ever thought I could be,' he said. 'I thought she had committed her heart to me. I had intended to speak to you about her future, as soon as we returned to London. But I had not thought it would be over breakfast.'

The Dowager relaxed and took another sip of tea. 'Your explanation is sufficient. I will tell neither Mr Leggett nor Comstock what has happened, unless Hope requests it of me. You have one week to either settle the situation with my granddaughter, or settle the matter of the entail. If either is incomplete at the end of seven days, I expect you to disappear from our lives, just as quickly as you arrived. Is that understood?'

'Yes, your ladyship.' As he stood and left the table, he could already feel the clock ticking.

Chapter Fifteen

Hope sat on the edge of her bed, waiting for the clock to strike one so she could return to London. At all costs, she avoided her own reflection, afraid to see the change that everyone else had noticed in her own face. She had considered and rejected the idea of staying behind in the country to lick her wounds and sending Mr Drake back with Charity. Though it might be more pleasant to avoid confrontation, it did not change the fact that this house no longer belonged to her.

And there was still the matter of the missing diamonds. Mr Drake's promise of help was likely as fleeting as everything else about last night. That left her with explaining their loss to the new Earl of Comstock. She could not imagine he would have been as personable as Grandmama thought him had he known the truth.

There was a knock on the door.

'Go away,' she said. He did not have to say a word for her to be sure it was Gregory on the other side.

'We have to talk.'

'No, we don't,' she said. 'Never again.'

He opened without permission, came in and closed it behind him. 'Then I have to talk and you must listen.'

'If you mean to apologise, do not bother. I do not wish to hear it.' She kept her eyes focused on the floor, not daring to look at him.

'I am not sorry about last night, if that is what you are referring to,' he said. 'I refuse to apologise for the most wonderful night of my life.'

'If it was so wonderful, then why didn't you speak when my grandmother wondered about it?'

'You did not give me a chance,' he said, then dropped to his knees in front of her so that it was impossible for her to evade his gaze. 'Just as I had no chance to refuse you last night, or in the library in London.'

'Are you suggesting that this is all my fault?' she said, trying to pull away from him.

He reached out to grasp her hands before she could escape. 'There is no fault. No one is to blame because we did nothing wrong. We love each other.'

'Do we?' Had he ever said so, before this moment? Or had she simply assumed that he must love her to do the things he did.

'I thought it was understood,' he said, giving her the same narrow-eyed look she was giving him. 'But after what you said to your grandmother, it seems I was mistaken. You talk as though you would still prefer to wed an earl.'

'Not *an* earl,' she said, yanking her hands free. 'The Earl of Comstock.'

'Now that you know he is everything you dreamed he might be, I am no longer worthy of you,' he said, standing up again.

'That is not true,' she snapped, averting her eyes so she did not have to look into his. To do that was like staring into the sun, blinding and confusing. 'There is nothing wrong with you. It is me.' She did not have the words to explain what had changed in her, but something had.

'Perhaps it is you,' he said. 'Did you not understand that we would be obligated to marry, after what happened last night?'

'Obligated?' she said. That was what she had wanted. To make sure he had no choice. But now that it had happened, it was an empty victory.

'Yes,' he said. There was a faint softness in his voice. 'You might be carrying my child. I am not capable of doing what was done to me and abandoning a son or daughter, allowing them to be raised by strangers.'

She had not considered the possibility of a baby. But neither did she think that a child would be the first thing on his mind when making the offer she had hoped to hear. Now that she had fallen, what she had thought would be an act of love was nothing more than a duty. She stood up and walked past him to open her door. She pointed to the hall. 'You may think we have to marry, but I have no intention of forcing you to wed me. Nor can you force me to wed you.'

Now, he looked baffled. 'No one is being forced to do anything. If, after what has happened between us, you do not want me, I cannot make you. And if there is a child...'

'There will not be,' she said, terrified for the future. What child would want a mother bearing the mark of licentiousness that her sister and grandmother had spotted so easily? 'I will not be with child. I refuse to be. I will not have it. Or I will and I will give it to you, since that is all that you seem to care about. Now please leave me alone.'

'You think I do not care about you?' He laughed. 'Hope Strickland, I care more for you than I have ever cared for a woman in my life.' His hands reached out to her in supplication.

She could feel herself weakening and turned away. 'I care for you as well.' The words sounded false, even to her. They were far too weak to encompass her true feelings which ranged from love, to fear, to confusion and back to love again. 'I care for you. But that does not make it right.' She walked to the door and opened it, praying that he would understand and leave.

He shook his head, amazed. 'Very well, Miss Strickland, I suppose I must thank you for changing a lifetime's assumptions about the world and my place in it. I have wasted far too long trying to be a better man than the father I never knew. I thought he abandoned my mother to bear me and die. But perhaps she sent him away for no reason, just as you are doing to me. You have taught me that in matters of the heart women can bc every bit as cruel as men.'

The four of them rode back to London in ominous silence. Or rather, three of them did. Charity disappeared into her book the moment she was seated, blissfully unaware of the tension inside the coach.

The Dowager was her usual self as she entered and sat down, smiling brilliantly and joking that she would enjoy playing chaperon for the young people. Still smiling, she took the seat next to Hope and gave Gregory a look that said if he as much as stretched a finger in Hope's direction, she would have him thrown from the coach and whipped by the driver.

Hope might as well not have been there at all. She was not just quiet; she hardly seemed to breathe. Nor did she move, staring straight ahead at her sister on the seat across from her for the whole trip.

Gregory tried to tell himself that it was better than the alternative. When a love affair ended, some women were prone to hysterical tears, or angry tirades. They went out of their way to make the parting as difficult as possible.

But not Hope Strickland. After hours of nothing, it would have been a relief to see any emotion at all. The woman sitting on the other side of the coach from him might have been a total stranger instead of the most passionate lover he'd ever known. It made him wonder if he had imagined the last week. He could see no sign on her face that she had been in any way moved by him.

It was not until they were alighting back in London that he could be sure she still remembered. He offered his hand to help her down and she hesitated as she took it. But it was not from fear or revulsion of him. There was something in her eyes that hinted at a fear of her own reaction. Her heart was not totally lost to him, if she had to fight the response to his touch.

But what did he feel when he looked at her? He looked after her as she moved across the pavement towards the town-house door. In a few steps, she might be out of his life, which would return to its comforting routine. Jobs would be started and completed. Clients would come and go. He would remain safe and unaffected.

Her rejection had hurt him, of course. But that was almost a novelty. He had been rejected by women before and had never experienced a pain like that caused by her denial during breakfast. He had gone to her room sure that a simple explanation would be enough to set things right. Surely a girl as proper as she was would see that a hasty marriage was the best protection for her honour. Instead, she had rejected him again. A part of him did not want to try a third time.

But then his thoughts had turned to his father again. He had always imagined a rake or a rogue who did not care about the pain he'd left behind when he left. But perhaps he was just a coward. Perhaps he had slunk away from the woman he'd loved and the family he might have had, because he'd not been brave enough to claim them.

He had formed his character with no other plan than to be different than someone he did not know at all. Perhaps that was why he'd fallen in love with the sort of girl who caused more trouble being good than any enthusiastic sinner ever had.

He hurried down the path until he was one pace ahead of her, blocking her way to the door. Then he smiled at her as he had when they were nothing more than client and employee. 'If it is convenient for you, I shall return tomorrow at our usual time.'

'Return?' she snapped. 'What makes you think I would wish to see you again?'

'We have one item left to retrieve,' he reminded her, pulling out the list that was still in his pocket. 'A Chinese vase.'

'You said you would locate it without my help.'

He shrugged. 'I was mistaken.'

'You are mistaken now.' Her voice was shrill as if the idea of seeing him again drove her one step closer to madness. 'I have no wish to see you, ever again.'

'I have no wish to force my attentions on you,' he said, as mildly as possible. 'But I have a job to complete. It will go faster, and I will be gone sooner, if I have your help.'

She paused for a moment, as if weighing temporary discomfort with eventual freedom. 'Very well. One day. If the search takes more than that, you must complete it on your own.'

'Excellent,' he said with another one of his

professional smiles to put her off her guard. 'We will do our best to settle the matter tomorrow.'

When Hope returned to the house, her grandmama was waiting just inside the door. 'Well?' the Dowager said, arms folded across her chest.

She stared expectantly back at the Dowager, wondering if, after all the stories she had heard about the foolishness of overly strict morality, she was about to receive a dressing down for her own fall from grace.

'You were speaking with Mr Drake,' the older woman said. 'Have you settled the problem between the two of you so I can book St George's for the wedding?'

'There is no problem between us,' Hope said, with a forced smile. 'He was employed by Mr Leggett to help us fix the problem you created. Tomorrow, we are going out to find the Chinese vase. Then his job will be finished and we will see no more of him.'

'What utter fustian,' her grandmother snapped. 'When I arrived at the manor, he was staring at you like a moonstruck idiot, unable to string two words together. And you looked like Eve, waiting for God's judgement with the apple still in her hand.'

Had it really been so noticeable? How was she to go about London with him? Or without him, for that matter? Was it something that would fade with time? Perhaps it could be washed away.

'Stop playing with your curls, Hope Strickland,' the Dowager snapped. 'If you are trying to look less guilty, you are making matters worse and not better. I'd blame your parents for dying before they could teach you to lie, but it did not seem to matter in Charity's case. She is younger than you and there are days when I cannot get a single truth out of her.'

'What am I to do?' she said at last, dropping the charade and pressing her palms to her face to hide the blush. 'I cannot see anyone looking like this. I certainly cannot meet the new Comstock. He will think me unchaste and want nothing to do with us.'

Grandmother shook her head in pity. 'Do not waste time worrying that men will want nothing to do with you. There are more than enough of them who prefer a girl with a glow in her cheeks and a twinkle in her eye. They are nothing to be afraid of. If you are walking out with the man who put it there, they will leave you alone.'

'I cannot spend the rest of my life in the company of Mr Drake,' she whispered.

'Well, not every moment. But once everyone is calling you Mrs Drake, it would be rather stupid of people to show surprise that he is bedding you.'

She turned back to her grandmother. 'For the last time, I am not going to marry Gregory Drake. He has not even asked me to.'

'He has not asked?' Surprisingly this seemed to bother the Dowager more than anything else. 'Then I shall have him dragged back here immediately to do right by you. And there will be none of this nonsense about punishing him for his hesitation by refusing.'

'That is not the problem at all,' Hope replied. 'He said it was his duty to marry me.'

'And so it is,' the Dowager said, with an exasperated shake of her head.

'But when I went to his room, I thought...'

'Did he invite you?' her grandmother said with a confused frown.

'He would never do something as dishonourable as that. Before we went to Berkshire he said that he did not think it wise for us to see each other again,' Hope explained.

'But then you insisted that he accompany you. And you went to his room when the household was asleep,' her grandmother said, her voice raising. 'You pestered the poor man until he succumbed, instead of giving him the chance to court you properly. And now you are complaining about the quality of his proposal.'

She had been so focused on her plan to marry Comstock that it had never occurred to her to flirt with him as Grandmama had suggested and allow things to develop slowly, as was proper. It was just as it had been at the ball, when she had resorted to theft, rather than asking permission. 'This is like the ink-well, only worse,' Hope said, closing her eyes in shame.

'My dear, I have no idea what you are going on about. But if it in any way resembles the current situation, please do not enlighten me. All I want to know from you now are your feelings towards Mr Drake.'

'I love him,' she said. But instead of making her happy, the words came out on a sob.

'Then stop torturing the poor man,' her

grandmother said with a sigh. 'You say he is coming back tomorrow morning to see about finding the vase from the hall?'

Hope nodded.

She glanced at the clock on the wall. 'It is growing late and he has probably had quite enough of our family for the day. We will not try his patience further. But if he is planning to return, he has either forgiven you, or can be persuaded to do so. Do whatever is necessary to mend the breach between you. I will make myself available in the drawing room, tomorrow between two and seven, should he wish an interview to discuss your future. But as I informed Mr Drake at breakfast, I will not see you moping about the house for more than a week. After that time, if you have not found a husband for yourself, I will arrange a marriage for you, just to get you out of the house.'

Chapter Sixteen

When she was through being badgered by her grandmother, Hope escaped to her room to find that the inquisition was not yet over. Her sister was waiting for her in her bedroom. Charity had seated herself upon the bed, propped herself up with every pillow in the room and spread her dusty books all over the coverlet.

'You have a room of your own,' Hope reminded her.

'Neither of us has a room,' Charity said, barely looking up. 'Have you forgotten that the Earl has arrived?'

Hope closed her eyes for a moment to let a fresh wave of panic wash over her, before opening them to stare back at her sister. 'If he is not here tonight, there is no reason for us to share this space.'

'Grandmama says he claims to have no need of the town house.' Charity frowned. 'Perhaps he does not understand that Parliament is in session and he must take his seat in the House of Lords. It would be rather foolish of him to stay at a hotel until the Season is ended.'

'Do not worry,' Hope said, bitterly. 'I am sure he will be along to evict us once he has a better grasp of the situation.'

'You mean when he discovers that the diamonds are missing,' Charity said.

Hope pushed her sister's books out of the way and sat. 'Who told you that?'

Charity had finally stopped reading long enough to look at her, with her usual expression of patient superiority. 'No one had to tell me anything. I have been playing with the whole set from the moment I was out of the cradle,' Charity replied.

'You were doing what?'

Her little sister shrugged. 'You and Faith would not share your dolls with me. You said I was too young. So I stole Grandmama's jewel case to play at being grown up.'

'You wicked little thing,' Hope said, before remembering that it was never possible to change Charity's character with scolding.

'Grandmama caught me at it. It made her laugh to see me decked in tiara and bracelets. She made me promise to put them back in the box when I was done and set aside the things she did not want me to damage. But those were the pieces that Grandfather had given her and not the diamonds. She had not a thought for the pride of the Stricklands. Do you not find that strange?'

'I am long past finding Grandmama's behaviour strange,' Hope said.

'Well, I did. When I was old enough to understand, I went to the library...'

'Quelle surprise.'

Charity ignored the jab. 'I searched for a book that would explain how to tell real diamonds from false. And it was then I noticed the scratches on the stones. Real diamonds are hard and will only be scratched by other diamonds.'

'You knew they were paste and you did not see the problem with it?'

'If it did not bother Grandmama, then why would it bother me?'

'Because our grandmother, the woman who

should be protecting us, is constantly doing things that put us in jeopardy. She steals things that do not belong to her and sells them without a thought to the consequences. If it did not bother her that the diamonds were false, it is because she was the one who took them.'

'Or perhaps it is because they were false when she received them, on her wedding day. And false for Great-Grandmother as well,' Charity said, unperturbed. 'Either she does not know that they are paste, or she has always known and has grown used to the idea. It does not matter, either way.'

'It matters immensely,' Hope snapped. 'It matters because we will be lying if we give false stones to Miles Comstock and present them as real.'

'We are not going to give him anything,' Charity said. 'They are already his. And it is quite possible that his auditor will know even less about diamonds than we do. He will open the case to see that all the spaces are filled, write it in his ledger, then lock them away again.'

'But when they are worn, everyone will discover they are false,' Hope said, horrified.

'No one has noticed as yet,' Charity reminded her.

'Because our grandmother is such a persuasive liar,' Hope said with disgust.

'Or ignorant of the truth,' Charity reminded her. 'It is possible, you know.'

'But unlikely,' Hope said.

'You, on the other hand, will definitely know. You are also a terrible liar,' Charity declared. 'This is why you are convinced that disaster is imminent. Because, as you have proven in the past twenty-four hours, you are physically incapable of keeping a secret.'

'Even if I can persuade Mr Drake to make another offer, I will have to rusticate until the wedding,' she said, closing her eyes in resignation. 'I cannot face anyone in this condition.'

'Fallen from grace?' Charity threw her hand across her face and collapsed on the bed in a mock swoon. She sat up immediately, as composed as ever. 'Stop being so dramatic and look in the mirror.'

'I do not wish to,' Hope replied.

'You cannot avoid it indefinitely. Look at yourself.'

Hope allowed one more moment of hesitation, then turned suddenly, in case the expression was something elusive that might hide if she took the time to prepare her expression.

She stared into the mirror, then stepped closer for a better look. The family was right. Something had changed, but what? Her hair was styled in the same way it had been yesterday. Her gown was not new. She had never needed rouge or powder, nor did she need it today. And then she saw it.

As Charity had reminded her, when it came to words, she had never been good at dissembling. But that did not mean that she went about with a Friday face when things were difficult. Problems were no easier to bear if one kept a pleasant smile, but one was spared the inconvenience of nosy strangers wondering what the matter was.

But today, it seemed she could no longer control her expression. The frown of confusion staring back at her was too real, as was the look of surprise. She had expected to find a brand of infamy. Instead, it was as if her emotions had been laid bare for all to see.

'I should probably marry Mr Drake,' she said and watched the radiant smile that followed the announcement. Though strangers might not guess what she had been doing last night, there was no hiding the fact that she was in love.

'At least you are no longer talking about becoming the next Countess of Comstock. You would be the last girl in the world I'd choose if I needed someone to walk about London in a paste tiara.'

'That is probably true.' It was also strangely cheering to free herself of the plan. 'But I must still meet with Mr Strickland to explain about the diamonds.'

'Or you could return to Berkshire and avoid him,' her sister said. 'You never need meet Miles Strickland at all, you know. There is no law that says we have to associate with family, if we do not wish to.'

'That is true,' Hope said, turning back to face her sister. It had never occurred to her that it would be possible to avoid a meeting. But if she withdrew from society, he might not bother to seek her out.

'If he does not marry immediately, we might be long gone from both his houses before he even thinks to ask about the diamonds, much less look at them,' Charity added.

'It is not as if he will be wearing a necklace and earbobs to Parliament,' Hope said, feeling not just better about the future, but almost happy.

'Then it is settled,' Charity said with a nod. 'If you cannot keep mum about it, you will avoid Miles Strickland and give up on the idea of becoming his Countess. If you marry, it must be to a man who solves your problems instead of adding to them and who can protect you from your excessively virtuous nature. And I could not suggest a better husband for you than Gregory Drake.'

Gregory's smile faded once he was out of sight of the Comstock town house. The Dowager had promised a week to set things right. While Lady Comstock might not plead his case for him, he did not think she would be working actively against him during that time.

But though she had allowed him a sennight, Hope Strickland had given him but a single day. There had to be something he could do to stretch that, so her temper might cool sufficiently to hear his apology. Before he had understood the magnitude of her problem, he had convinced her of his ability to work miracles. If ever one was needed, it was today.

It might take a handful of diamonds to earn him more time and the three-carat stone to set things right between them.

He began his search at the jeweller that had provided the leather case for the Comstock parure. After speaking to the proprietor, he went to another more dubious shop. From there, he went to a place so obscure that it had no name on the window and no number on the door. He left, satisfied, a short time later.

Next, there was the matter of the new Comstock. He'd had no real opinion of Miles Strickland when he'd still been at sea. But now that he was on land, Gregory had developed a genial hatred for him that had only grown with the Dowager's description of a prince among men. As long as Hope remained Miss Strickland, her cousin was a threat to their future happiness. Something would have to be done.

Gregory's agent at the dock confirmed that Miles Strickland, travelling alone except for his little dog, had arrived five days ago in Bristol, then, after travelling to London with the Dowager, his luggage had been directed to the Clarendon. It was near to supper and the food there was excellent. In Gregory's opinion, there could be no better time to investigate the competition for Hope's attentions.

When he arrived in the hotel's dining room, there were few empty chairs. He signalled for the assistance of the porter, scanning the diners already seated. In a far corner at a small, poorly lit table, he saw a man with shoulders so sloped that they did not just seem to bear the weight of the world, they looked as if someone had dropped that weight from a great height.

He gave a nod of his head in the direction of the fellow and held a coin where the porter could see it. 'Is that man an American?'

The servant nodded. 'Mr Strickland from Philadelphia.'

'And did he request that unfortunate spot, or did you force it on him?'

'He said he was not interested in company.'

'Well, we do not always get what we want, do we? Take me to him.'

As they approached, Gregory called out, 'Potts! Old fellow, I have not seen you since Cambridge. Lud, but this place is a crush tonight.' He dropped into the seat opposite the new Earl. 'You do not mind if we share a table, do you?'

From the front, Strickland looked as miserable as he had from the rear. Perhaps the Dowager had not exaggerated when she'd spoken of her visit to a sick cousin. His skin was sallow, probably the result of poor diet, hard travel and a passage spent cooped up below deck. From the poor fit of his suit, there appeared to have been a sudden loss of weight.

Fortunately for Gregory, Strickland had not yet acquired the aloof nature of a peer, nor did he realise that a man of his importance should never have been interrupted by rude strangers. A word to the staff and the scribbled title 'Comstock' on the hotel register would have been all the protection he needed. Instead, he was left blinking in surprise, as if unsure of what to do about the intrusion. Finally, he said in his strange, flattened accent, 'I am sorry. You are mistaken. I am not the man you are looking for.'

Gregory blinked back at him, feigning surprise. 'An American? Then you cannot be Potts, though you are the spitting image of him from the back, at least.' He glanced around the room, shaking his head. 'But this place is still packed to the rafters and you have one of the few empty seats. Would you mind terribly?'

'Not at all,' Strickland replied with a look that said he was not sure whether he minded, but did not see what he could do to stop it.

'Gregory Drake,' he said, offering a hand.

'Miles Strickland,' the Earl answered, taking it.

'You are clearly new to England, Mr Strickland. How do you find it?'

Comstock took a deep drink from the glass in front of him. 'Utterly mad, Mr Drake. I am not surprised that my country wanted no part of it, if it chooses its governors based on their last name rather than their abilities.'

'I assume this means you will not be staying with us long.'

Now Miles Strickland looked even more miserable and poured the last of the wine from his bottle before draining his glass in a single gulp. 'If I could find the money for it, I would be on the first boat back to Philadelphia.'

Gregory tried to contain his surprise. 'How fortunate that we should meet, Mr Strickland. You sound like a man who might be in need of my services.' He reached into his pocket and produced a card.

The Earl stared at it for a moment, puzzled. 'You describe yourself as a solver of problems. Is this a common thing in England? I am sure I have never heard of such in Massachusetts.'

'I am the only one that I know of,' Gregory said, trying not to brag.

Strickland gave a gloomy shrug. 'That is very interesting. But the problem that has befallen me is nothing a stranger can solve. Once you hear it, I doubt you will want to help me, even if you are able.'

'That is what they all say,' Gregory replied with a smile. Then he raised a hand to signal the porter. 'Let me buy us another bottle of this excellent wine. After a nice chop and a few more glasses, you shall tell me all about it.'

The meal came, then the bottle. And then things got interesting.

Chapter Seventeen

The next morning, Gregory arrived at the town house as he always did, on the stroke of ten. But he'd arisen earlier than usual to prepare for this visit than he had the others. The creases in his cravat were as sharp as the razor that had shaved him. He wore his best coat and new gloves and had spent more time adjusting the angle of his hat than a sailor spent with a sextant.

He was not a vain man. But if this turned out to be the last time he saw the woman he loved, he wanted her to remember him at his best. And if it was not the last time? Then everything about the day must be perfect.

Hope was waiting for him in the hall of the town house, as she always did. Had she taken care with her appearance as well? It seemed so. Her bonnet was new and matched a green-velvet coat that would be more appropriate on Bond Street than the neighbourhoods he had been taking her to visit. Even the errant curl was under control today, tucked safely under her bonnet.

'Are you ready to accompany me, Miss Strickland?' He offered his hand to her.

He felt her tremble as she accepted it. 'Yes, Mr Drake, I am ready. Let us finish this, shall we?' The arrogance that had coloured her voice on the day they'd met was gone, replaced with an unexpected gentleness. And had he really seen a sparkle in her eye as the veil had dropped to shield her face? It had looked almost like a tear.

She was sitting across from him in the carriage now. He could not tell whether she looked away from him, or gazed at his face as steadily as he was gazing at hers. It did not matter. He would not allow her to do either in silence. At this late date, each word he could wring from her would be deemed a step towards regaining her love.

'Did you sleep well, Miss Strickland?'

The veil on her bonnet rippled, as another shudder ran though her. It must have been embarrassment, for she whispered, 'You are not supposed to ask things like that, Mr Drake.'

She had not called him Gregory, but neither had she snapped at him. Things were going better than he'd expected they would. 'Would you have preferred that I asked how you find the weather?' He pulled up the shade and glanced out the window. 'It is a lovely day, is it not, Miss Strickland?'

There was a moment of silence, as if she could not decide how to answer the simplest question. Then, she said, 'I am sorry, Mr Drake. After all that has happened between us, I do not think I know how to make polite small talk with you.'

'What do you wish to do instead?' He had several suggestions, none of which were appropriate for broad daylight or a closed carriage, even with the shades drawn.

'I wish to apologise,' she whispered. 'It was very improper of me to come to your room in the manor. And I behaved even worse the next day, when Grandmama caught us there together. I have treated you abominably.' She expelled the words in a single rushed breath and they were barely loud enough to be heard over the rattling of the carriage wheels.

'Perhaps you have,' he agreed and heard a surprised gasp from behind the veil. 'But I cannot blame you. I should not have allowed anything to happen between us. While I am working, it is a point of pride on my part that I treat the families of the men who hire me with the utmost respect. With you, I have broken that rule.'

'I did not mind,' she whispered.

'I did,' he said. 'And if it were possible to go back to the day we met, things would be different.'

'But since we cannot, do you think it might be possible to start again, now?' Her voice was so quiet that he almost could not hear it.

'I would like that very much,' he said. 'But we must wait until the list is complete.'

'What difference will that make?' she asked.

'Once it is done, I will no longer be in the employ of your family. Then, if you still want to know me, we will meet at properly chaperoned social gatherings, as other ladies and gentlemen do. We might be friends.'

'Or more than friends,' she said, then gasped again as if she'd realised that it was not her place to make such a claim upon him.

He smiled at her to assure her she had not been too forward. 'We will start fresh. This afternoon, after we have found the vase.'

'I would like that,' she said. He could not see her smile, but he was sure it must be there.

'I am glad to hear that, Miss Strickland,' he said, falling back on professionalism to hide the pleasure he felt at her response. 'But first we will find your vase.' He pulled a piece of paper from his pocket. 'I have compiled a list of likely dealers in ceramics and fine porcelain that might have purchased it from your grandmother. Were you able to get a more exact description from her?'

'I do not need her word for the vase. I know perfectly well what it looks like,' she said. 'And I can also assure you that it was not in any of the shops we have already visited.'

'Do not worry. I have no intention of wasting your time with those places, Miss Strickland,' he said, turning to the second page of the list.

'In fact, I do not see why you cannot just grab the first vase we see, as long as it is about three feet tall and of a Chinese design,' she added.

'But that would be dishonest,' he reminded

her, trying not to smile at her eagerness to be done. 'And you told me on the first day that such a casual approach would be insufficient.'

'That is true,' she said with a disappointed sigh.

'Do not worry, Miss Strickland,' he said, forcing his smile. 'I will take you to every last shop in London, or to China itself, if necessary. But we will return the correct vase to the correct place in the correct house.'

Once they arrived at the first stop, they fell back into the familiar pattern of their searches. Gregory made polite conversation with the shopkeeper while Hope examined the displays, searching for the vase. When she found nothing, she touched his arm, shook her head and they went back to the carriage.

They tried again. And again. In their past excursions it had taken no more than a few stops to find the missing item. But today, they progressed down the extensive list that Gregory had made, with no luck at all. After the progress they had made towards a truce, he did not want to see the afternoon spoiled by simple bad luck.

'I hope you do not think I am leading you

in circles. I swear to you, I thought we would find something by now.'

'I am sure you are doing your best,' she assured him. 'Perhaps we will find it at the next shop.'

When they stopped again, he held his breath and uttered a silent prayer, for there was a huge Chinese vase sitting in a corner of the shop. She went to it immediately, running her hands over it with familiarity.

Gregory went to stand behind her, looking over her shoulder. 'Is this it?' He could not keep the excitement from his voice, but she was too preoccupied to notice.

'The colour is right. The one I remember had the same pattern of flowers running up the side and the red dragon twining in and out of them.' She pointed down at the base. 'And I have tripped more than once over the cast-iron stand.'

She ran her fingers over the rim and shook her head. 'This is smooth,' she said. 'There should be cracks.'

'We are looking for a cracked vase?' He did his best to contain himself, but she turned and caught him stifling a laugh.

'And I suppose you are about to suggest that

we break this one.' Her response was frustrated, but not angry, as if the humour of the situation was not lost on her.

'I will do so if it makes you laugh again,' he said softly. 'But I promised you we would find the right vase and I always keep my promises. Come. There are other places we can search.'

They visited three more shops and he found it harder to smile with each failure. If he wanted to assure her of his ability to care for her, he did not want to appear to be a failure. 'I am beginning to wonder if you are trying to destroy my perfect record,' he said, trying to make light of it.

'I have told you from the first that I did not believe you could not solve every problem,' she said.

She was speaking of the diamonds again, but since last he'd seen her something had changed. It was as if she was resigned to their loss. He gave her an encouraging smile. 'Sometimes, there are solutions you have not even imagined yet.'

'If you are suggesting that I run away with you and avoid the issue, you needn't bother. No matter what happens, I will not leave my family when they need me most.'

Her declaration caught him off guard. She had been as eager to start again as he was. But then, it had been as if he'd walked towards an open gate, only to have if it swing shut in his face. As usual, the Stricklands were on one side and he was on the other. Neither a night of passion nor a proper daytime courtship was likely to change that. 'Of course not,' he said, still numb.

The coach was stopping at the last shop on his list and it was almost a relief. If he was to fail, let it be soon. Then he would give her his other piece of news and see if it was more disappointing to her or less. 'I do not really expect to find anything here,' he said with a shrug. 'We have not visited it before because I did not think there was a chance of finding anything of value. But I will not give up until I am sure all hope is gone.' And he was closer to that than he had ever expected to be.

Despite the cold in the February air, the shop's front door was propped open and smoke billowed out into the street. Once their eyes had adjusted to the dim light inside, they could see that the majority of it came from a tiny fireplace in the corner and the few smouldering lumps in the grate that were barely worthy of the name coal. The rest came from a long pipe the proprietor puffed, filled with the foulest tobacco in London.

'Hello, Tibbett,' Gregory said, holding a handkerchief to his nose, attempting to block the smell.

'Drake!' The man put down his pipe and the smoke wreathing his head cleared enough to reveal his jagged-toothed smile. 'What can I help you with today?'

'We're looking for a vase,' he said, smiling back. 'A posh one. Wide like a pot and so high.' He held out a hand.

'Don't have much call for that,' Mr Tibbett said, frowning and pointing. 'What I got is there, in the window.'

Gregory gestured to Hope to look for herself, though he had seen nothing close to the duplicate she had shown him earlier. But before she could reach the alcove that served as the display window, she stumbled over a heavy metal something that was being used as a stop to hold the front door open.

He was at her side to catch her before he'd even had time to think. That was how it had been on the first day and how it would always be. No matter what she said or did, today, tomorrow, or in the past, he loved her. He could not help but care.

She paid no attention to his touch, too focused on the thing at her feet to notice his help. She pulled free and crouched, hauling the doorstop away and letting the door swing shut with a bang behind her. She swung her arm wide, nearly knocking off his hat as she held the thing aloft.

She struggled to carry it to the counter for the ornamental cast-iron stand must have weighed at least a stone. As Gregory watched in amazement, she set it in front of Mr Tibbett with a loud clunk. 'It is here. It must be for I have stubbed my toe on this so many times I would know it anywhere.' Apparently, she no longer needed his help. She pushed past Gregory, pulled up her veil and spoke directly to the proprietor. 'Sir, can you help us? There is a vase that belongs with this stand.' She held out her arms in an *O* shape to indicate the size. 'It is nearly waist-high and decorated with chrysanthemums and a dragon.'

'A big red snake, you mean,' he said.

'Rather like that,' she allowed. 'But I think, actually...'

'I have been meaning to throw the pieces

away for ages. But the old lady what brung it promised she would return for it.'

'That is the one, I'm sure.'

'Pieces?' Gregory repeated, alarmed.

'I never would have taken a thing in that condition. But she insisted...'

'My grandmother can be most persuasive,' she agreed. 'And just as she promised, we have come to collect it and to pay you whatever was promised.'

'What condition were we speaking of, precisely?' he interrupted.

Since what he thought was obviously unimportant to her, she ignored Gregory's question, as did Mr Tibbett. 'It's in the back room,' he said, gesturing them further into the shop. When Gregory stopped on the other side of the curtain that separated storage from shop he called, 'No, further than that. You'd best light a candle. I do not waste the money on them, since there is nothing of value there.'

'The thing we have spent all day searching for has no value,' Gregory repeated to her as Hope pushed past him again, reaching for a taper and going back to the stove to light it.

She walked past him yet again, light held aloft, trying to see to the backs of the dusty shelves. 'There it is,' she said at last, pointing towards the corner, at the pile of broken china.

'It was in one piece when it arrived,' Tibbett said a little defensively. 'But when I tried to move it...'

She waved his protestations away. 'Do not concern yourself, sir. It was broken long before it ever came to you. It was in the hall that we used for footraces when we were little girls. Someone bumped into it at least once a year.' She looked embarrassed. 'But I was the one who finally knocked it off the base. I glued it back together and crossed my fingers. Grandfather caught me at it, of course. But his punishment could not change what had happened.'

'I was told no such thing when I took it,' Tibbett said, his eyes narrowing. 'I'll still be wanting the original price for it,' he said.

'And I have no intention of wasting my client's money on something you were too lazy to chuck in the bin,' Drake replied with an equally steely gaze.

'Pay the gentleman, Mr Drake,' Hope said, stooping down to gather up the pieces of the last Comstock heirloom. 'I will put it back together again when we get back to the town house.'

'Forgive me for asking, Hope. But are you mad?'

Apparently, the answer was yes. At the sight of her precious vase, she could not even be bothered to lecture him about his rudeness. She was on her knees, ready to scoop the broken pottery into her spread skirts.

He seized her wrist to stop her and pulled her to her feet. 'If you are intent on having it, let me do that. You will cut your hands.'

She gave him a militant look as if ready to remind him that it was not his place to dictate to her like a lover or husband. He glared back to tell her that she could just as easily have ordered him to do what he'd offered to do, since, apparently he was nothing more than a dustman for the peerage.

Then he turned back to Tibbett. 'I'll pay the original price if you throw in a trunk to carry the pieces.'

'The pot, a crate and a sack,' Tibbett countered.

'Done,' Gregory said with a sigh. 'And the use of your coal scuttle and a brush, to sweep up the pieces. He opened his purse and counted out the bills the man requested and recorded the amount spent in the little notebook. Once that was finished, Gregory turned back to the pile of broken pottery, stooped down and began piling the bits into a sack. Then, he carried it to the carriage.

Hope was already waiting for him inside it.

As they set off for the town house, he spoke. 'You are not seriously planning to leave that mess for the new Comstock.'

'I will try to put it together again,' she said and appeared puzzled that he would even ask. 'It belongs to his estate. My great-great-great-grandfather...' She paused, counting on her fingers and trying to remember generations. 'At least, I think it was that many greats. The Fifth Earl. He was involved in the silk trade with the Orient. This was a gift from a Chinese princess. It is almost priceless.'

'If by that you mean without value, I wholeheartedly agree,' he said. If they had seen another vase just like it, the stories she had been told were likely rubbish, just like the vase.

'You think an antique porcelain vase from China has no value?'

'That used to be a Chinese vase,' he said,

pointing at the pile of shards in the box at their feet. 'Now it is nothing.'

'It is simply damaged,' she said, gathering her skirts to be clear of the grime on the box at her feet. 'When I was a child, I was not as careful as I might have been. Accidents happen.'

'I do not doubt it,' he said. 'But then we clean up after them and move on with our lives. Rational people do not turn London upside down to find the contents of the dustbin after the junk has been carted away.'

'A little paste, a little patience and it will be good as new,' she said, with a smile that was almost as fragile as the porcelain had been. 'At least, it will be as good as expected. It is centuries old.'

Centuries old. Just like her family was. And there was the problem. She could not seem to separate the things from the people. 'Can you put flowers into it?' he asked, folding his arms.

'Why would I do such a thing?'

'Because that was its intended purpose.'

'I seriously doubt that,' she said. 'It is far too large for a bouquet.'

'What is it for then?' he urged.

She stared at it for some time, trying to figure out what its purpose might have been. 'I think it might have been a cistern. Or a very large chamber pot. Or perhaps it was meant to hold an ornamental fish.'

'Well, it is useless for any of those things now. It will never hold water again. But I can find you any number of new pots just as good,' he said. 'The one we looked at several shops ago was nearly the same.'

'But it will not be ours,' she reminded him.

'It was not yours in the first place,' he reminded her. 'Nor was it your grandmother's, when she sold it. And the new Earl would not know it from a hundred other similar vases I have seen in shops all around London. He would likely be grateful to have it replaced so that at least one thing in his home does what he expects it to do.'

'You cannot possibly understand,' she said. 'We are attempting to maintain the history of the family.'

'Of course not,' he said with a grimace. 'Since I have no family to claim me, I am forced to live in a nice house with modern conveniences and undamaged goods. In turn, your cousin has come all the way from Philadelphia to live in a house full of useless and broken items, kept for the sake of posterity. Do you not see the madness of this plan? If you cannot, I suspect Comstock will notice it when he arrives at the manor.'

'You have no idea what the new Earl will or will not think,' Hope said, growing more annoyed by the minute.

'Haven't I?' Gregory said, trying to be patient, so she might find the truth on her own. 'I am not the one who has been building Miles Strickland into some kind of saviour who will fix all the problems of the family with a wave of his hand.'

'No, you haven't. You tried to make him into a villain because you were jealous,' she reminded him.

'I did,' he agreed. 'Nor did I tell you that the other half of the task put to me by Leggett was to disabuse you of the notion that marrying him would solve all problems. He even gave me permission to lie to you, just the way I did.'

'So you blame my brother-in-law for your bad character?' she said, shocked. 'Did he tell you to seduce me as well?'

'I blame no one but myself,' Gregory said,

his face hardening. 'I refused his suggestion and planned to reason with you instead. But at the ball, I was willing to throw away my principles for one moment of your attention. Today is proof enough that reason would have been pointless. I will never be able to change the mind of a woman who chooses to ignore what is right under her nose.' He pointed down to the box at her feet, wishing that she could see it as he did.

'I have no idea what you mean,' she said, honestly puzzled.

'Have you never wondered why, when it came time to rob the entail, your grandmother chose the things that she did?'

'Because she was selfish and did not think of the future difficulties it would cause,' Hope said, without thinking. And that was the problem. She did not dare think. She was afraid to.

'I have been to the manor with you,' he said, walking her through the steps to the truth. 'A single chair from the dining room would be worth more than all the things we have recovered. Can you not see what she has done?'

'She stole things that did not belong to her,' Hope said, stubbornly. But there was something in her eyes that flitted on the edges of awareness, crying to her that something was not right. He had but to get her to listen to it.

'She did not take a chair because to do so would devalue the set. Instead, she sold rubbish. Dented candlesticks. Paintings too ugly to hang. Broken vases.' He waved his hand. 'And that abomination in the box. Comstock was right. It is a wonder that we common folk do not rise up like the Americans did and wrest power away from the nobles, for no sane family would want to preserve such detritus, much less punish one who disposes of them.'

'You have spoken to my cousin,' she said, taking the wrong message from his last words.

'Because I wished to confirm that what I suspected was true,' he said. 'It was and he has my sympathies. The poor fellow has only just begun to realise the misfortune that has befallen him.'

'He is heir to an earldom,' she said, shaking her head against what she must know was the truth.

'And head of a family that cannot pay their bills,' Gregory said, making no effort to blunt his tone.

'If Grandmother had not taken the diamonds, he would not have reason to worry,' she snapped.

'If you search your heart, you will know that that cannot be true,' he said. 'One of the smaller stones in the tiara would have been enough to run the estate for a year. The lavalier would have been enough for a decade. If she had sold off the diamonds, why have you been scraping by with half a staff? Why has the Dowager resorted to pawning small things that no one would miss so there might be food on the table?'

She was shaking her head, as if she still did not want to believe. He could see the truth rising in her mind like a bubble in stagnant water.

Before she could speak, he did, so she did not have to say the truth aloud. 'There were no diamonds. There never have been. If ever they existed, they were sold off generations ago to support a decaying system that is finally about to fail. God help Miles Strickland, who has traded a perfectly good life in America for ruin and heartache with a family who refuses to admit to themselves or the rest of the world that they are poor.'

'Poor.' She said it very softly as if the word itself were the problem and by speaking it the situation would be made real.

'You have kept hope alive by thinking that it was temporary,' he said. 'That all problems would be solved when the heir arrived. That as long as he was happy with the three of you, he would set things right and you need never worry again. But what good will it do you to marry the Earl of Comstock if there is no money at all to unencumber?'

'We are poor,' Hope repeated, as if still trying to grasp the thought.

He nodded encouragement. 'I have the proof of it here.' He pulled a piece of paper from his pocket and handed it to her. 'My job was not finished until I kept my promise to you and settled the matter of the diamonds. You know I would not leave you without keeping my promise.'

'You have found them?' He could see the hope coming back into her face like rising colour.

It broke his heart to have to dash it again. 'I found an explanation for their absence. I know nearly as many jewellers in London as

I do pawnshops. I made enquiries after we returned to London.'

'You gave away our secret to strangers,' she said, dazed.

He shrugged. 'The ones I deal with tend to have a certain flexibility of morality. I know far too much about them for them to speak of what they know of me.'

'Dealers in stolen goods,' she said.

'And those skilled at the duplication of entailed family jewellery,' he said. 'Many families come forward at some time or other with a need for paste copies to thwart highwaymen. My friends do not care whether the reasons they give are true or not.'

'It is not just Comstock?' she said, still stunned.

'Lord, no. Half the families in London are lying to the other half about how much money they have.'

He should not have told her this way, without any warning at all. Her eyes had grown round and her brow was furrowed in confusion. She looked like a child on an unmoored boat, watching the world she knew slipping away, with no idea how to save herself.

'But back to the matter of the diamonds,'

he reminded her. 'When we returned to London, I set about tracing them. The shop I visited has been in business for generations and makes almost as much money for their forgeries as they do with real gems.' He tapped the letter again and pressed it into her hand. 'They also keep excellent records.'

She stared down at the paper in front of her. 'Someone requested stones exactly like the ones in the family jewels.'

'And you can see, from the date referenced that it was during the Civil War.'

'They have been gone since 1645,' she said, staring at the paper.

'Perhaps they hid the real stones from the government. Or perhaps from the rebels. Or they sold them to cover some age-old debt. I am sorry I cannot produce them for you.' He reached out to take her hand. 'But this should be sufficient documentation to prove to anyone who cares that the loss of them was an old family secret and not improper management by your grandparents.'

'I have been worrying about a problem that did not exist,' she said.

'You have done what you have done because of lies that have been told to you for your entire life,' he said, trying to keep the anger from his voice, lest she think it was directed at her. 'If you had told me the truth earlier, I could have saved you much pain. Now that you know it, you must see that you cannot bring back the past, as you remember it. It is gone.'

'But if there is no money, what is to become of us?' she said, still stunned.

'That is up to you,' he said. 'I have no title. But I have money and a house, and on my worst day I can provide a better future than Comstock ever will. Let me do that for you, Hope. Let me care for you. Let me love you.'

After all her talk earlier in the day about starting anew, now that the moment had come, she said nothing.

They had arrived at the town house and it seemed foolish to wait in the carriage once the servants had opened the door. He hopped out and helped her to the ground. But today, she seemed as broken as the Chinese vase. As her feet touched the pavement she stumbled, unable to support herself.

And as he had before, he caught her before she could fall, putting a hand under her elbow to help her keep her feet. For a moment, things were as they had been, when she had trusted him with her life and her love.

But when she looked up at him, she still seemed as confused as she'd been in the carriage. There was no sign that she had heard the offer he'd made.

With his free hand, he signalled for a footman to take the box of broken china. He helped her into the house, not releasing her until he was sure she was able to stand on her own. 'Shall I call for a servant to bring you a restorative?' he asked. 'Tea, perhaps? Or brandy?'

'No. That will not be necessary,' she said. She was still deathly pale, but she raised her head in a fair imitation of the proud beauty he had met just a week ago.

'You do not have to worry,' he said. 'No matter what happens, you will not be alone.'

'Of course not,' she said, with a faltering smile. 'I have my family and they have me as well. I cannot abandon them when life is at its most difficult, you must see that, Mr Drake.'

'Of course,' he parroted back, fighting the desire to shout the truth back into her white face. Perhaps it was because he had no family, but he did not understand at all.

'I must speak to Grandmama about what you have told me.' She was glancing absently about the room, as if the Dowager were nothing more than another misplaced item to be found and put in the correct spot. 'And Charity, of course. I do not know if there is anything we might do to ease the burden on our American cousin. But we must try, mustn't we?'

'Of course,' he said again. It should be some comfort that, if she held him to blame for the night at the manor, she had forgiven him as he'd hoped. But she had forgotten him as well. Though he'd offered her the new start she had wanted, only a few streets from where they stood, she could not imagine a life outside this house any more than she could imagine that a trip to China might be more interesting than playing with a vase in the manor hallway.

She had made her choice and it was not him.

Now, it was as it had been on the first day they'd searched. His job was complete and it was time for him to leave. Yet though she had just dismissed him, he was standing there like an idiot, waiting for some signal that he was still welcome. Did he honestly expect her to thank him for turning her life upside down?

So, just as he had on that day, he fell back into his expected role of consummate professional. 'And now, Miss Strickland, we have come to a parting of the ways. As Mr Leggett requested, all the items on your grandmother's list have been found and returned to the estate. I have encouraged you to think of a future that does not include a marriage to your cousin, but I am under no obligation to stand in the way of a match, should the two of you wish to make one. At least, with my research into the history of the Comstock diamonds, I have proved that it is not necessary to offer yourself as some sort of matrimonial sacrifice to appease his anger. Take him the letter and explain all. I am sure he will be as interested in the matter as you are.'

She gave him a hesitant nod.

He continued. 'Given certain things that have occurred between us, I understand that you may not wish to offer a favourable reference for my services. But do not concern yourself that any part of this incident will come back to you as gossip. I was hired for my discretion. No word of it shall ever pass my lips. And if you need them in the future, do not hesitate to call on me.'

The words spooled out of him, as they always did, like the final lines of an actor exiting the stage. With minor variations, it was the same speech he always gave when the job was finished and there was nothing left to do but collect his payment and move on. He delivered them with the same patent smile he had given her on the first day, the one he used on strangers.

This was the moment when his clients often thanked him. The words were almost as gratifying as the money. They would have been even more so today. He needed some small scrap of assurance that what had happened between them was something profound and not the dream it had begun to feel like. But Hope Strickland had mastered the art of ignoring the obvious long before he'd met her. Why should she admit to feelings that would prove inconvenient in the future?

He turned to go, then paused, his hand on the door handle, and turned back to her, unable to resist one more look, one last attempt to repair the damage he had done by falling in love with her. 'Do not believe what you have been told about the fragility of a lady's honour. Any man who deserves your love will not fault you for your past, should you decide to admit to one. You are an extraordinary woman, Miss Strickland. I wish you well.'

Then, he crossed the threshold, closed the door and was alone again.

Chapter Eighteen

Hope sat at the table in the kitchen with a pot of paste and small brush, surrounded by uneven shards of china. It was fortunate that the pieces were large. There did not seem to be any missing. Her makeshift repair would do until the vase could be properly restored.

Of course, if what Gregory said was true, there would never be a time when that could be done. A single failed crop or bad storm could impoverish the tenants and take the estate down with them. Her cousin would have far worse things to worry about than a broken pot.

Still, she could not help trying. That was what the Strickland sisters did, after all. They made the best of what was given to them. They did not give up when things looked hopeless. They soldiered on without cutting corners or breaking rules.

According to Charity that made her tedious and impossible to live with. Was that how she had seemed to Gregory? Perhaps if she had been more reasonable from the beginning he'd have courted her as other gentlemen did, dancing at balls and flirting politely.

And she'd have ignored him. For all she knew, they could have met months ago, if she'd had eyes for anyone but the man coming from America. If she had been honest about the diamonds, with him, or with Charity, she'd have learned the truth earlier and made different choices. She'd made things worse by assuming she could handle everything alone.

Had things been different, she might have accepted his offer. She was sure that was what he had been attempting to do in the carriage. She loved him, of course. But love was not all that mattered.

When she had gone to his room, she'd assumed that the financial problems the family faced would be solved with the appearance of the Earl. The loss of the diamonds would be embarrassing, but not critical. Comstock might be placated and allowances would be restored.

But the family problems were even worse than she had imagined. She could not simply walk away and abandon Charity and Grandmama to poverty. Nor did it seem right to leave Miles Strickland. Whatever he had been expecting when he had crossed the ocean to take his rightful place, it could not have been what he had got. She could not love him, for Hope doubted it was possible to love two men at once. And try as she might, she loved Gregory just as much as she had, that night in the manor. But she owed Mr Strickland some part of her affection, if only because of their shared heritage.

Grandmama had hinted that their American cousin wished to make an offer. He needed someone who knew the details of the estate and understood how to be a countess. She would be that for him, if he needed her to. As long as she kept her heart to herself and did not wear the Comstock diamonds, everything would be fine. Not happy, of course. But she must not let personal happiness stand in the way of the natural order of things.

From the corridor to the muddy back garden came the sound of singing and the happy clopping of the Dowager's pattens on the tile floor.

Hope set the brush aside and listened. She had not heard Grandmama singing since before Grandfather had died. As usual, the woman's mirth was ill timed, but Hope would not begrudge her a moment of it.

The Dowager swept into the room and dropped on to the fireside bench to remove her wooden overshoes. 'My dear Hope, why are you wasting time inside when the robins are singing in the trees and the air is as crisp as a summer apple?' But all movement stopped when she saw the broken vase. 'Good heavens. Whatever are you doing with that?'

'Trying to repair it,' Hope said. Just as she had been trying and failing to fix everything else about the family for the better part of the month. Even though no one had asked her to. Nor had they welcomed her help.

Nor was she appreciated today. 'Do not be silly, Hope. We no longer have to bother with such things. It is Comstock's vase, now. Let him be the one to mend it.'

'It is not fair that he should be left to solve

problems we created,' Hope said, automatically. Did she always sound so tiresome?

'Solving problems created by others is the stock and trade of the peerage,' her grandmother replied. 'If it is not the Crown, it is the tenants. If it is not the tenants, it is the family. It is always something, my dear.' She thought for a moment. 'The new Comstock will have to be rather like your Mr Drake.'

'He is not my Mr Drake,' Hope said hurriedly.

But the Dowager ignored her and continued. 'But I suspect Mr Drake is better paid and sleeps more soundly at night. You chose well.'

'I did not choose him,' she said glumly. Not even when he had given her a second chance to do so.

'Then you should be glad he chose you. If I had picked a different husband, I might have had a much easier life, but it would not have been as happy. I loved your grandfather quite fiercely and he loved me in return. The burden of being Comstock was easier because we shared it.'

'I thought you were happy.' Was nothing as she thought it had been?

Her grandmother touched the locket at her throat that held a tiny braid of her husband's hair. 'I was as happy as it was possible to be given the truth of our circumstances.'

'Gregory... I mean, Mr Drake says that we are poor.' She'd said it in a whisper, for it seemed as if, spoken aloud, it would suddenly become true.

Her grandmother laughed. 'Poor as church mice, my dear. Albeit, mice that live in a cathedral and not some small country parish. The Comstock earldom has not had two coins to scratch together since your grandfather was a lad. It is why there was no settlement to provide for us, once he died. There was nothing left to give us.'

'Why did you not tell us?' Hope said, shaking her head.

'What could you have done, other than to marry well and escape? Faith has done so already. Soon, you will be gone as well. If I'd told either of you, you'd have thought it necessary to stay together for the good of the family.'

'And for Charity,' Hope reminded her.

'As she has been telling you for years, Charity can manage for herself,' the Dowager replied. 'It is time you listened to her. But you and Faith needed a push to leave the nest and I provided it.'

'You sold these things for us,' Hope said, touching the broken pot in front of her.

'I could not send you to Almack's in a borrowed gown,' the old woman said in a reasonable tone. 'I took the least of what we had to shops where no one would ever see it again. It was just barely enough to launch you all and keep meat on the table.'

Hope reached out and took her hand. 'We never knew.' Or perhaps she did know. She just hadn't understood.

Her grandmother's answering smile said that she had understood for both of them. 'Do not worry about the past. The new Earl has come now and I shall finally be free.'

'Free?' Hope whispered, confused.

'Free of the houses, the debts and the worry. Of trying to make something out of nothing, all the while pretending that we were happy for the honour. And free of the guilt over those ridiculous diamonds.'

'You should not have let me badger you over them. Why could you not tell me the truth of that, at least?'

'Tell you the biggest secret of the Comstocks?' She shook her head and laid a finger on her lips. 'Only the Earl and Countess know the truth and they pass it to the next generation. Of course, that means that each Countess must wear a paste tiara with a smile on her face and pretend that nothing is the matter. I wore select pieces on special occasions in the darkest of venues. But each time I did I was in agony that someone would guess the truth.'

'How will we ever tell Miles Strickland?' she asked.

'We do not have to. I already did. I blurted it out the minute we were alone together.' The Dowager fanned herself with a hand and sighed as a woman did when removing stays that had been laced tight for hours. 'He was very nice about it, all things considered. He arranged for a settlement for me and promised me the use of the dower house, if it can be repaired sufficiently to be habitable.'

'That was very kind of him,' Hope said.

'Too kind, I think.' She smiled sadly. 'He underestimates how much money will be needed to fix the place. It will be far less expensive if I take his allowance and live abroad.' If the old woman had been happy before, now she was overjoyed. 'I shall go to Paris, perhaps. Or Rome. For the first time in years, I shall see something other than a London Season. And no one shall require me to keep up appearances.'

Hope winced and looked down at her stinging hand. She still held a piece of the vase and a drop of blood was forming on the pad of her finger where she'd gripped it along the sharp edge.

Her grandmother reached out and took it from her, offering a handkerchief in its stead. 'You girls will do as you want, for you were never ones to listen. But you will be better off if you do not try to fix things that cannot be mended. Let it all go and you will be happier for it.' She held the piece of vase out over the tiles and released it.

Hope gasped again, as the perfectly mendable scrap shattered to slivers so small there would be no hope of putting them together again.

The Dowager wiped her hands together as if satisfied with a job well done. 'Sometimes it is not the clean break that saves us. Life is messy, Hope. Embrace it.'

'But what about Charity?' she said again.

The Dowager gave another shake of her head. 'I have never met a girl so capable of fending for herself.'

Everything had been done. There were no secrets to hide from or reveal to Comstock. Grandmama did not need her help. In fact, she was so eager to leave her grown granddaughters to their own devices that she could not contain her excitement. And when it came to being ruled over and lectured by an older sister, Charity had made her opinion quite clear.

Hope was not wanted. She was not needed. Not in this family, at least. There was still someone who had loved her, had needed her and still might have her if she could unbend enough to ask for his forgiveness. But to go to him, she would have to let go of the past.

Without another word, Hope grabbed a piece of the vase, closed her eyes, dashed it to the ground and listened to it shatter. Then, she fumbled on the table, found another piece and sent it after the first, savouring that crash as well. This time, she opened her eyes, reached out her arm and swept the remaining pieces to the floor. Perhaps she was still not brave enough to look at the disaster at her feet. But the sound echoed in her heart, like the clank of falling shackles.

Her grandmother was right. Freedom was sweet.

Chapter Nineteen

Now that she was decided, Hope did not bother with pattens or cloak and bonnet. She did not even bother to clean up the mess she'd made by throwing china on the floor. Instead, she shouted an apology to the maids in the kitchen and rushed out the door.

Once outside, she did not walk sedately, as a lady should when strolling through the streets of London. Instead, she lifted her skirts to an immodest but efficient level for running and tore down Harley Street, turned at the next corner and ran the three streets to the Wimpole Street address that Gregory had given her.

There she stopped to stare up at the house, momentarily afraid to go further. It was not proper to visit a gentleman unescorted. But if she considered the things she had done with Gregory, she was probably no longer a lady. Her desire to be bound by convention had kept her from doing things she actually wanted to do for too long. She could not waste another minute. She took a deep breath to settle her nerves and grabbed the knocker, letting it drop.

She was still out of breath from running when a butler answered, staring down at her with the sort of distant confusion that one got from servants confronting the unexpected.

In his moment of hesitation, she could not resist craning her neck to gaze past him at the hall. Everything within sight was new, clean and elegant, just as she had imagined a house owned by Gregory Drake would be.

It did not give off the sense of inherited wealth and power that Comstock Manor did. Nor was it cosy, as she remembered the vicarage being. But it did not smell musty and it did not leak and when things broke Gregory could afford to have them mended or replaced. That she could be mistress of a house was yet another revelation.

The butler cleared his throat. 'May I help you, miss?'

She smiled up at him. No. She beamed, for he was just one more example of the efficient household in her future. 'Is Mr Drake in?'

'I am sorry, miss. The master is currently away from town.'

For a moment, she had trouble comprehending the words. When they had parted this morning he had promised that he would be there if she needed him. And yet he was already gone. Had it been nothing more than the sort of empty courtesy that he offered in parting to all his clients?

If she had learned anything from the last week, it was that she must make an effort to understand others rather than demanding a perfection that even she was not capable of maintaining. He had promised he would be there for her. If he was not at home, there would be an explanation for whatever happened. She simply had to find him and ask.

'Where did he go?' she demanded, leaning to the side to peer around the servant, half-expecting that Gregory would appear out of nowhere as he always seemed to when she wanted him.

This time, the butler moved to block her view. 'I am not at liberty to say, miss.'

'Then when will he be back?'

'He did not say, miss. If you wish to leave a card, he will be informed of your visit when he returns.'

'No.' She backed away from the door. 'No, thank you. I will find him myself.'

The butler was looking at her as though she might run mad in the street. Since that was how she had arrived at the house, she should not be surprised.

'It is all right,' she assured him, still backing away. 'Perfectly all right.'

He closed the door slowly. She was sure, as she turned and hurried back down the street, that he watched her from the window. But was the butler the only one to do so? Gregory might be waiting behind a curtain as well, having informed his staff that, should Miss Strickland appear, he was not at home to her.

She could not believe that. He had promised if she came to him he would not turn her away. He would not have said it if he had not meant it. But that left the question of where he might have gone in less than a day and how she might find him if he had given no one permission to tell her.

She smiled. To find Gregory Drake, she

would have to think like Gregory Drake. If he wanted to find a person, he would search systematically using whatever clues he could find. Of course, he had a well-developed network of contacts all over London. She had not as much as a mutual friend to ask.

She knew his last employer. She could write to her sister and tell her to ask Mr Leggett to divulge anything he might know about the man he had hired. But that would take weeks, at a minimum. And since Gregory had completed the job for her family, he was likely to be working for someone else, already.

Of course, I offered my services...
And suddenly she knew.

The trip to the Clarendon was but a short ride through the city. But today, it seemed like the longest journey of Hope's life. She took the time to return to the town house and let Polly comb the tangles from her hair. She put on her best visiting gown, bonnet, coat and gloves. Beyond that, she took no more care than she would for any other visit. She had spent weeks preparing herself for the man she was about to meet. Now that the moment had arrived, it was not as much anticlimactic as totally unrelated to the things that truly mattered to her.

All the same, she was nervous. Once she arrived at the hotel, she gave her calling card to a porter and asked him to deliver it to her cousin with her wish to speak to him in the dining room. Then, she sat down to wait.

A short time later, a gentleman appeared in the doorway, scanning the room as if searching for her. If she had been expecting a family resemblance, she was disappointed. He was taller than her grandfather had been and thinner as well. His hair was dark. It seemed almost black against his skin which was unnaturally pale. His eyes were a not particularly vibrant green.

Her grandmother had called him handsome. While she did not disagree, his appearance left her strangely unmoved. Her head was too full of another man to appreciate him. Once he had recovered his health, her cousin would devastate the maidens of Almack's. She wished them luck.

But of one thing she was sure: he did not look as she expected an earl to look. There was some undefinable thing missing from him that she'd taken for granted in her grand-

father and his peers. Was it arrogance? Pride?
Or merely the confidence of a man who con-
trolled the world around him for further than
his eye could reach. Miles Strickland did not
appear to be a master of his universe. He
looked as though he was not sure where he
belonged.

All the same, he intimidated her. Now that
the opportunity had finally come to meet the
heir, all her practising was for naught. She
rose as he drew near, and dropped into a wob-
bly curtsy. 'My Lord Comstock.'

When she raised her eyes to smile at him,
he looked thoroughly uncomfortable with
both her deference and greeting. 'Please,' he
said wincing. 'Sit down, Miss Strickland. We
are family, are we not? Surely the formality
of a title is not necessary.'

'As you wish, my lord.' She resumed her
seat.

'And the honorific is not necessary, either,'
he said, wincing again before sitting in the
chair opposite her. 'I am not totally sure it is
even appropriate yet. There must be some papers to be signed. They cannot just expect...'
His voice trailed off, confused again. 'To call
me Mr Strickland would be rather confusing.

Would it be too inappropriate for you to call me Miles?'

Probably. But if it was what he wished she would accede. She smiled again, though she could still not manage the dazzler she had planned for him. 'If you wish, I shall call you Miles. And you must call me Hope.'

He nodded, relieved. 'Very well, Hope. It is good to meet you. If you have come to welcome me, I am surprised that you did not bring your sister with you. I looked forward to meeting both of you.'

'Actually, I had not planned to impose myself on you, until invited,' she said.

'I see,' he replied, disappointed. 'And what changed your mind on the subject?'

'My friend, Mr Gregory Drake, mentioned that he had seen you,' she said. 'I went to visit him today and found he has travelled from town without leaving notice of where he was going. I wondered if, perhaps, he might have mentioned his destination to you.'

And now he was surely wondering about the manners of English women and whether it was normal for them to ask impertinent questions of people they had just met. But, if she had shocked him, he hid it well. 'Yes, Mr

Drake. We dined together the day before yesterday and again this afternoon.' He gave her an appraising look. 'He speaks most highly of you.'

'He does?' She had given him no reason to, but it was nice to know.

'Yes. Especially after a few glasses of brandy. When he left me today, he was somewhat the worse for drink and under the impression that I was likely to marry you. In fact, he strongly advised it. He says you are a capital choice and that it makes a great deal of sense for us to wed, for the sake of family solidarity.'

'Oh.' As usual, Gregory Drake was working very hard behind the scenes, like Cupid's own stage hand, to see to it that she got the things he thought she wanted.

'Your grandmother seemed to like the idea as well. When she met me in Bristol she took great pains to remind me that you and Miss Charity are not married and it is my responsibility, as head of the family, to see that you do so. But not just any man will do. Nearly everyone I have spoken to since I arrived seems to assume that it would be for the best if I stepped up and offered.'

'I see,' she said, even though she did not want to. Had it been just a few hours ago that she was prepared to accept? Now, she would have to find a polite way to refuse.

'You wouldn't happen to be in love with Mr Drake, would you?' Miles said with a sympathetic smile.

'Yes?' she said. Her voice quavered, making it sound almost like a question. 'Yes,' she said, more firmly, and smiled as her strength returned.

He sighed. 'That is good to know. Because, you see, while everyone thinks it is a good plan for us to wed, I can't say that I'm sold on the idea. You seem very nice, of course. And you are very pretty. But we do not know each other at all and what kind of a marriage would be made of that?'

'That is true,' she said, amazed at the flood of relief she felt to be rejected by the man she'd waited for for months.

'If you should happen to marry someone else before I've had a chance to court you, I would find that most convenient.'

'I am not sure he still wants to,' she said. 'He asked me, but I refused him.'

Miles sighed. 'What is wrong with the pair

of you? You seem quite besotted with each other. Make sure he offers again. By week's end, if that would be possible. That damn Prince is after me to declare myself and I need a reason to say no.'

'The Regent,' she said, horrified.

'Solidarity of the state. Heirs. Something like that,' Miles Strickland said, shaking his head. 'He wants to make sure I marry the right sort of girl and not an opera dancer or an American.' His lip curled in distaste. 'Back home, we do not have to worry about the government meddling in our personal affairs. James Madison does not know me from Adam's off ox and that is just the way I like it.'

'The Regent expects us to marry,' she said again, pointing between the two of them.

'But we are not going to,' he reminded her, smiling. 'You are going to marry Greg Drake, as soon as possible.'

'But I do not know where he is,' she said, helpless.

'Is that all?' The Earl let out a relieved puff of air. 'I sent him down to Berkshire. Or up. I am not sure where it is, exactly. But I have a house there.'

'To the manor,' she said, shocked.

'I had requested an audit of the entail. But though everyone in this country has been telling me what they expect of me since the day I arrived, no one actually listens to what I want. Except for Greg Drake, that is. He seems to be a dead useful fellow, able to write in a clear hand and smart enough to count the sheep, or whatever it is I have.'

'He is at the manor,' she repeated.

'I'm told it's not far. But I haven't seen it myself. Feel free to take my carriage. Apparently, I have several of them,' he said.

She was gone from the table before he could finish the sentence.

Chapter Twenty

Hope rode the whole way to Berkshire on the edge of the forward-facing seat, as if it was possible to arrive sooner just by wishing it so. She did not bother to look out the windows to chart their progress for it was nearing sunset when they'd set out and would be full dark by the time they arrived.

Nor had she bothered to pack, or even to stop at the town house to tell her grand-mother where she was going. She suspected that, when she did not appear at dinner, the family would guess who she had run to. In any case, it was too late for them to object to the thing they had been encouraging her to do all along.

When the carriage arrived at the manor, she was out of it the moment it came to a full stop and hurrying into the house. The servants looked at her in alarm, embarrassed to be unprepared for her late visit and ready to find who or what she was searching for. She held a finger to her lips and shook her head. 'It is a surprise for Mr Drake.'

If it concerned them that she had arrived unchaperoned at bedtime to surprise a man who was supposed to be there as an agent of the Earl, they said nothing. But then, there must have been gossip after her last visit. They had to suspect by now that he was more than just another family employee.

To silence any doubts, she added, 'I was sent by the new Earl with a confidential message for him.' She tried not to smile, remembering what the message was. But the statement brought her the privacy she wanted for the staff would not dare risk intruding in case she had told them the truth. 'Do not bother to direct me. I will find him myself,' she added to send the last curious footman back to his business.

Of course, that left her with the task of locating him. She paused at the foot of the stairs to listen for the sounds of business on the main floor. She heard none, but that was hardly unusual. It was a large house with thick doors. She was used to the sound of silence echoing in the high-ceilinged halls. She also knew that there were forty rooms to search.

She smiled. It was not the first game of hide and seek she had played here, but it was certainly the most gratifying one. To catch him, she would have to think like Gregory, again. If she was completing an inventory, a systematic approach would be the best. Would he work from cellar to attic, or attic to cellar?

Neither, she decided. For while he might proceed in an orderly fashion in someone else's house, Gregory Drake was a romantic. There was only one place he would be, if he had just arrived.

She went to the first floor, walking down the hall to the bedrooms. It made sense that he would be given the same room he had occupied on the last visit. And it was even more likely that he would be overcome by memories once he entered it. That was where she would find him.

The door was open and she looked in to find him sitting on the edge of the bed, facing away from her, staring out the window. He had placed the candlesticks that belonged in the dining room on the side table next to the crystal inkwell from the study. Between them was a ledger with the beginning of a list detailing the contents of the room. The last item he'd recorded was an Aubusson rug, crimson with gold border, seventeen by eighteen feet.

'You might add that the weave is exceptionally good,' she said, glancing down at the tidy lines written without break or blot. 'One can walk on it and you will not hear a footstep.' She had proved the fact. By the time he turned to her, she was practically at his side.

He sprang to his feet and spun to face her, before regaining control and giving her the same polite smile he'd worn when they parted. 'Miss Strickland.' He bowed. 'I did not expect you.'

'I gave you no reason to,' she reminded him. 'When we parted this morning, I doubt you thought you'd ever see me again.'

'That will be at the discretion of Lord Comstock,' he said, the consummate professional he had been on the first day they'd met. 'Is there something I might assist you with?' The mask slipped and his brow furrowed. 'Do you need my help?'

She nodded. 'I went to your home to find you, but you were not there.'

'I did not think you would need me so soon,' he said, his frozen smile returning. 'As you can see, I took another position with your family.'

'And you have removed the candlesticks from the place I put them,' she said, running a finger down the length of one.

'I needed the light,' he said, then added, 'And they reminded me of you.'

'Cold and unbending?' she asked with a smile.

He shook his head. 'When we found them. The look on your face that day. I think that was the moment I fell in love with you.' He stared at her for a moment and she felt the heat of it touching her skin. 'Now will you tell me what brings you here? If it is some task left uncompleted, I will discuss it with you anywhere but in this room.'

'I broke the vase,' she said.

'That was long ago,' he reminded her. 'You know where to find a better one. Should you wish to buy it you do not need my help.'

'No. Today. This morning. On purpose. I threw the pieces on the floor and smashed

them to bits. I suspect they are in the dustbin
by now, for there was nothing left of them
worth saving.'

'I told you so when we found them.' He
sounded faintly annoyed. But there was something else there, too. Something encouraging.

'I have decided you are right,' she said. 'We
can go back and buy the one we saw that had
no cracks in it. No one will know the difference.'

'How will you keep the secret from Lord
Comstock?' he asked.

'Very poorly, I suspect,' she said. 'If he asks
me, I will admit I broke it and that there was
nothing more that could be done.'

'That is surprisingly sensible of you,' he
said, his eyes widening. 'And what do you
mean to do about the matter of the diamonds?'

'He already knows,' she said. 'Grandmother
told him immediately upon his arrival. She
has decided to leave him to his fate.' Though it
was probably not ladylike to gloat over someone else's misfortune, she could not seem to
stop grinning. 'And though he seems very
nice, I do not think there is anything I can do
to help him.'

'You have spoken to him?' he said, embarrassed.

'To find you,' she reminded him. 'He said you told him he should marry me.'

'I thought it was what you wanted,' Gregory said.

'I know what I said. I want to know why you said it.'

He rubbed his forehead, feigning confusion. 'I am still feeling the effects of the brandy I drank after we parted. By the time I spoke to Comstock, I was in no condition to speak to a future employer. It was an act of mercy on his part to send me here. But I seem to recall informing him that you were hoping for a proposal.'

'I have been hoping for that for some time,' she said, giving him a significant look. 'A decent one that has nothing to do with honour or duty.'

Apparently, the hint was lost on him. 'By God, if you prefer the man, take him. But I will not say another word on the subject of marriage until I am sure you've had the offer you were expecting when we met. Accept him or refuse him, then notify me of the results so I might know if my heart will ever be my own again.'

She sat down on the bed. 'Do you think I would be here, if I'd accepted the offer of another man.'

'Where you are concerned, I have no idea what to think any more,' he said, sitting down on the bed beside her. 'Now tell me what I want to know. Did he offer, or not?'

'He does not wish to offer. I do not want to accept.' She smiled at him. 'I do not want to settle for a man as ordinary as an earl. I would much prefer a man who is truly exceptional.'

'You deserve nothing less,' he agreed. 'As I said before you are an exceptional woman. But what does any of that have to do with me?'

'I think you know,' she said.

'Please reassure me.'

'Comstock was relieved to find that I loved you. You are his employee now and I am to tell you that you must marry me within the week so that everyone will stop bothering him about me.'

The corners of Gregory's mouth twitched. 'I am, am I? And how much will he pay me to do it? For I do not recall marrying you as being part of our original agreement.'

'You said before that you were too foxed to remember what was said,' she replied. 'But we all know that he has nothing to offer you. If you still want me, I am afraid you will have to take me without a dowry. I am poor, you know.'

'If I still want you?' The smile he gave her as he said it was the same one he had worn the last time they'd been alone in this room, as if she was the most wonderful thing he had ever seen. 'I have never stopped.'

Without another word, he slid from the bed and dropped to one knee. 'But if you will not have me, Hope Strickland, I don't know what I shall do, for I cannot manage to let you go.'

'Nor I you,' she said, smiling back and taking the hand he held out to her and kissing it.

With his free hand, he reached into his pocket and produced a ring, captured her hand and slipped it on to her finger. 'It is not as big as the Comstock diamond, but unlike them it is genuine.'

She spread her fingers, admiring it. 'It would not matter if it were real or not, as long as we can be honest about it. How long have you had it?'

'I found it in one of the shops I visited,

when searching for your family jewels.' He shrugged. 'I had meant to offer it to you yesterday morning. But things did not go as planned.'

'Things are going much better now, I think,' she said, standing and pulling him to his feet.

'I agree.' He pulled her forward and wrapped his arms around her waist. 'So Comstock wishes us to wed within a week? That is very close to the amount of time your grandmother allowed me to secure your hand.'

'And when you promise to do a thing you never fail,' she reminded him. 'Since I do not want to spoil your perfect record, I think it best that we abide by their wishes.'

'It is too late to marry you tonight,' he said, with a yawn. 'And I have not completed nearly as much of the inventory as I had hoped to.'

'Then I will help you,' she said with a smile. 'We have already done the rug. I think, next, we must inventory the bed.'

Chapter Twenty-One

Charity Strickland sat comfortably in her favourite chair in the Comstock town-house library. The rest of the family insisted that it was more pleasant than the one in the manor. But that was precisely the problem she had with it. She liked her privacy and she could not seem to get any here.

She could hear footsteps coming down the hall and Hope paused in the open doorway. As she had since the morning after she'd seduced Mr Drake, she looked so radiant that the room seemed to grow brighter when she smiled. Charity set aside the journal she had been readying and gestured her to enter. 'Have you come to scold me about my plans to return to the manor again?'

'You know I have not,' Hope replied.

'Grandmama says that you are worried about the Earl's dog.'

'The poor thing is used to company,' Charity replied. 'And it is a very large house for such a small animal.'

'Your argument will be more convincing if you allow him in the library with you,' Hope replied. 'Be sure you have prepared a bed for him there by the time the Earl arrives.'

'As long as he does not chew on the books, he can have his choice of any chair in the room.' She gave Hope an encouraging smile. 'But never mind that. You have come to tell me about your impending marriage to Mr Drake.'

Hope laughed. 'Why is it impossible to surprise you?'

'Because as I have told you before, you are easier to read than these journals. Our ancestors had atrocious penmanship. Now tell me about the wedding, and I promise I will not try to guess the details.'

'We are eloping,' Hope whispered, taking both her hands and squeezing them. 'Running away to Scotland this very afternoon. Of course, it is not exactly a proper elopement, since we have Grandmama's blessing and the Earl's as well.'

'Only you would try to find a way to elope properly,' Charity said with a shake of her head.

'But it is possible that Faith and her husband might object.' She sounded almost hopeful of the idea. 'I do not know what Mr Leggett will think when the man he hired to help us runs off with me.'

In Charity's opinion, if James Leggett had a problem with this, then he should have had better sense than to send the perfect man for Hope. 'I do not think it is any of their business who you marry, as long as you are happy.'

'It will be even less so if we are properly married by the time they return,' Hope said with an evil grin.

'You are displaying an impressive level of rebellion, Hope Strickland,' Charity said. 'I applaud Mr Drake's corruption of your high standards and hope that it continues after your marriage.'

Hope bent to kiss her on the cheek. 'Even if it does not, I will not have as much time to bother you about your future as I did. If

Grandmama intends to travel, it will be up to the Earl to find you a husband.'

'Or I shall have to find one for myself,' Charity said.

'And for that you insist you shall need money.' Hope pulled a paper from the pocket of her gown and handed it to her. 'And that is why I am giving you a wedding gift, in advance.'

Charity unfolded the paper, and read the letter from the jeweller, describing the purchase of the paste stones. 'How very interesting. Wherever did you get it?'

'I asked Gregory to search for the jewels and he found the information in just one day.' Hope was beaming again. 'Isn't he amazing?'

'Indeed,' Charity agreed.

'And the most fascinating thing is he can find no evidence that the stones were sold. They must still be in the house somewhere.'

'What wonderful news!' Charity said. 'The next Countess will not have to parade around in paste if the Earl can find them and replace them in their settings.'

'I have an even better idea,' Hope said, then went to check the hall lest they be overheard. When she saw no one, she returned to

Charity's side and whispered, 'You must go back to the manor and hunt for them yourself. You know the house better than any of us. Find the stones and keep one or two of the smaller ones for yourself, just as you joked of doing before. Use them for a dowry, or travel as Grandmama is going to do. There will be little hope for you if you remain in the country. And I know you do not want to live with your sisters.'

'Keep stones for myself? That is a positively wicked idea, Hope. Those stones belong to the entail and I would never think of doing such a thing. I am going to pretend that you never said it.'

'Suit yourself,' Hope said, raising her arms in surrender. 'But I have learned from experience that there is such a thing as being too moral.'

'It's about time,' Charity muttered, then smiled at her sister to prove that there were no hard feelings.

Hope smiled back and for the first time in ages she did not seem the least bit upset that she did not obey.

'Enjoy your elopement,' Charity said. 'And everything that comes after.'

Hope's eyes went wide. 'When we return, I shall go to the manor and tell you all about it.' She giggled. 'Scotland, that is.'

'Or you can write to me,' Charity said, glancing towards the door. 'I hope that Mr Drake means to take you on a honeymoon of some sort. Do not delay it for my sake.'

'I am sure Gregory would not mind,' Hope said. But from the faraway look in her eye, the offer to return had been nothing more than courtesy.

'Do not let me keep you,' Charity said, making shooing motions towards the door. 'It is a long way to Gretna Green.'

Once Hope was finally gone, Charity sat down with a sigh of relief and rang for tea. It was good to see both sisters properly settled and to be left alone to bask in the glow of her grandmother's loving neglect.

Some girls might have been bothered by the lack of attention. But as the youngest of three, Charity had been waiting a lifetime for it.

She glanced down at the letter Hope had brought her, still on the table next to the sofa. It was kind of Mr Drake to have gone searching on his own and very clever of him to have got this far without her help.

She had needed to give him so many clues to the winning of Hope that she had begun to worry he might be a touch slow. But then Hope had needed help as well. But his success in this and his eagerness to help boded well for her sister's future. Charity had wanted her second brother-in-law to be both smart and kind, just as Mr Leggett was.

Of course, she also wanted him out of the way. The longer his inventory could be prevented, the more time she would have to look for the stones. She'd spent months reading old journals, making pages upon pages of notes, measuring walls and comparing architect's notes with old floor plans. As soon as Hope was gone, she could pack up her books and return to the country so that her search could begin in earnest.

Though Hope had suggested she keep a diamond or two, by Charity's calculations it would take four of them to catch a husband, but five if she wished to remain unmarried. It begged the question if the gowns and folderol that were deemed necessary to attract the masculine sex were an effective use of the money.

She smiled. It did not really matter as of

yet. She need not make a decision until after she had her hands on the diamonds and had found a man worth marrying. But of one thing she was sure: she would not spend a minute of her life sitting on the edge of a dance floor waiting for the future to come to her. After all, the Lord helped those who helped themselves.

* * * * *

COMING SOON!

We really hope you enjoyed reading this book. If you're looking for more romance, be sure to head to the shops when new books are available on

Thursday 28th June

To see which titles are coming soon, please visit
millsandboon.co.uk

MILLS & BOON

Coming next month

ONE WEEK TO WED
Laurie Benson

Charlotte's gaze dropped to Andrew's lips just as a giant boom reverberated through the hills. They both turned towards the house to see more colourful lights shoot into the sky and crackle apart.

'I'm thinking about kissing you.' He said it in such a matter-of-fact way, as if the idea would not set her body aflame—as if the idea of kissing this practical stranger would be a common occurrence.

Charlotte had only kissed one man in her life. She never thought she would want to kiss another—until now. Now she wanted to know what his lips felt like against hers. She wanted him to wrap her in his arms where she would feel desirable and cherished. And she wanted to know if his kiss could be enough to end the desire running through her body.

He placed his gloved finger under her chin and gently guided her face so she was looking at him. The scent of leather filled her nose. There was no amusement in his expression. No cavalier bravado. Just an intensity that made her believe if he didn't kiss her right then, they both would burn up like a piece of char cloth.

It was becoming hard to breath and if he did in fact kiss her there was a good chance she would lose consciousness from lack of air. But if he didn't kiss her...

She licked her lips to appease the need of feeling his lips on hers.

He swallowed hard. Almost hesitantly, he untied her bonnet and put it aside. Gently, he wrapped his fingers around the back of her neck, pulling her closer, and he lowered his head. She closed her eyes and his lips faintly brushed hers. They were soft, yet firm, and she wanted more.

Continue reading
ONE WEEK TO WED
Laurie Benson

Available next month
www.millsandboon.co.uk

LET'S TALK
Romance

For exclusive extracts, competitions
and special offers, find us online:

f facebook.com/millsandboon

⊙ @millsandboonuk

🐦 @millsandboon

Or get in touch on 0844 844 1351*

For all the latest titles coming soon, visit
millsandboon.co.uk/nextmonth